www.albedo1.com

Issue 50

	Beautiful Friend	Robert Neilson	5
	Cargo	David Murphy	8
	Cattle	Konstantine Paradias	9
	The Nape of Marie Antoinette	Ian Watson	13
	Pandora's Mailbag	Todd McCaffrey	30
	Step Right Up	Roelof Goudriaan	34
	Walking on Water	Tais Teng	39
	The End of the Road	Juliet E. McKenna	45
	The Vanishing Act	John Kenny	50

Things Change | 1

Reflections

Editorial

It's taken 30 years but Albedo One has finally reached the end of its journey. I guess none of us ever dreamed that the magazine which sported a black and white cover without even artwork, would last so long and transform into something of which we could be, justifiably I hope, very proud. Everyone involved with this final issue has supported us with their writing or editorial help over the years and I am delighted to have them aboard at the end. In my head, this final issue was always called *Beautiful Friends* because that was how I thought of those who contributed their time and talent over the years. *Albedo One* was never a 'real' paying market. Writers were never paid more than a token amount and often worked for free. The editors got Christmas dinner and a few pints at the end of the year. But this project was never about money and it could not have survived without our Beautiful Friends.

John Kenny and Dave Murphy were there at the beginning and have reappeared from time to time and for this final hurrah. Also there at the very beginning was Phillipa Ryder around whose kitchen table the first plans were made. Roelof Goudriaan joined us early on, and has stuck it out right to the end even though he has been living in Belgium for the past eighteen years.

But we have never been purely Irish. I have to take this opportunity to thank the Milford crew who provided the most thankless task of reading the slush pile for several years. Kostas Paradias has read for us for many years from his home in Greece and I have never met him, but will be eternally grateful for all his excellent work on the slush.

I doubt Ian Watson and Todd McCaffrey have anything in common other that the fact that they are professional writers and acted as judges on the Aeon Award short story contest (sometimes referred to as the Ian Award as he was with us for so long and from the outset of the contest) which we ran for many years. Another full-time professional who gave her time to the cause was Juliet McKenna who helped out as a judge on the Aeon and wrote a regular (as regularly was our intermittent schedule allowed) book review column. Over the years the Aeon Award had too many judges to mention them all individually but we will always be grateful to them. One final mention must go to our first ever judge, the wonderful, and much missed, Anne McCaffrey, whose generosity to Irish and international fandom knew no bounds.

So, thank you to all of our beautiful friends and I hope that they remember us as fondly as we do them.

Terminus Est.

Beautiful Friend

Robert Neilson

Careers, like wooden legs, often run in families. I'm a journalist probably, because my father was a journalist. Not that he was a particularly good role model; he disappeared when I was seventeen. But the hook was already planted. I had been working for the local newspaper during holidays and after school since I was fourteen. Making tea, sweeping floors and running errands. For my seventeenth birthday the editor gave me my first reporting assignment: a sea-angling competition. My furrowed brow said, what do I know about fishing. The boss said, "Sink or swim." And I've been swimming ever since.

I have asked my mother why my dad left us. She told me we'd talk when I was old enough. Guess I'm old enough. A week ago she sent me a compact disc. It contained an unfinished story by my father. The accompanying note simply stated, *Finish It*. A woman of few words, my Mum.

Dad was a music journalist, worked for the old *Melody Maker* back in the day. I wondered why she thought the story would appeal to me. But I hoped it would answer my questions about his leaving, so I opened the disc. Which is why I'm writing this. Mostly my stuff is simply bookends to what he wrote: he called it Beautiful Friend. It still seems like a great title to me.

My editor threw a manuscript onto my desk. "Right up your alley, Bernie" he said, closing the door on his way out. I thought I detected a grin, possibly a smirk, but I turned the manuscript and read the byline. It was by Mick Dulvey. He had worked on *Melody Maker* in the Sixties and Seventies. I know him slightly. He was still there when I came aboard. Drank like a fish. Knew everybody in the business, from roadies to management to superstars. But he knew his way around a story. And what I read was a hell of a story.

He heard the nine hundredth rumour about Jim Morrison still being alive. Except this on was from a source he trusted. Someone who had known Morrison. Someone with no skin in the game and nothing to gain. So Mick Dulvey headed off to Costa Rica to see for himself. It was 1979. *Apocalypse Now* had just hit cinema screens. He headed upriver by boat to a flyspeck town on the Caribbean coast called Tortuguero. At every bend in the river he felt like Marlon Brando might be lying by the riverbank. All that was needed to complete the Vietnam image was a few explosions. Had Coppola shot it here on this river? No, he was pretty sure the shoot was in the Phillipines. But it could have been here. River, jungle, cheap labour, close to the States. Could have been perfect.

Tortuguero was a town of well under a thousand souls. None of them were rock stars or even white Americans. He asked questions in poor Spanish. Was told the white guy he was looking for was in San Francisco. By more than one of the inhabitants. Assholes.

It turned out that San Fancisco was the unofficial name of a tiny enclave across the river. Maybe 200 hippies and assorted fellow travellers and refugees. Unofficial because officially San Francisco didn't exist. The area was a national park and the hippies had been thrown out more than once. But they kept coming back and the local officials ran out of energy and ignored the illegal settlement. And that, apparently, was where Jim Morrison had fetched up.

Mick Dulvey found him pretty easily. Morrison wasn't really hiding out any more. Mostly, people had stopped believing he was alive and had stopped looking for him. Señor Jim had a hut at the back of the settlement. Everyone in San Fran knew who he was and where he was and didn't mind sharing their knowledge. He found Morrison sitting on a bentwood rocking chair under a woven palm umberella, smoking a joint.

"Smells like good stuff," Dulvey said by way of breaking the ice.

Morrison held out the joint, a smile creasing his mouth and eyes. That smile just before a cough. He exhaled, coughed, waved vaguely at the step in front of his hut, said, "Sit."

Dulvey took a long blast on the joint; reckoning it would be rude not to. "Honoured to meet you, Jim. Mind if I call you Jim?"

Morrison grinned. Ran a hand across his bald head. Smoothed his beard. Accepted back the joint. Looked hard at Dulvey. Seemed confused. "Don't hear English much, out here."

"Mind if I ask you a few questions, Jim?"

Morrison took a toke, squinted through the smoke at the journalist as though trying to remember if he knew him from before. Looking uncertain as to how he should answer. If he should answer. He looked at the joint. It had burned down to the roach. He dropped it onto the bare earth at his feet and ground it out under his sandal. Nodded his head. Ran a hand across his pate again. He spoke slowly, as though he had to think before letting each word past his lips. "Knock yourself out, friend."

Dulvey asked a lot of questions. "You

He asked questions in poor Spanish. Was told the white guy he was looking for was in San Francisco.

mind if I take notes?"

Morrison smiled vaguely. Held his hands wide in a welcoming gesture that Dulvey took as acquiescence. He wrote down the exact answer to very few questions.

"Why did you go into hiding, Jim?"

"Needed peace. I dropped out. It was a thing to do back then." He scratched his belly and stared off into the distance.

"How did you fake your death?"

"Doc was a friend." Morrison tapped the side of his head. "Knew I was on the edge. He kinda prescribed a break. Pam was supposed to follow on. She never did. Don't know why. Heard she died a coupla years later."

"1974," Dulvey supplied.

Morrison nodded sagely. "Kinda lose track of time down here. 1980 yet?"

"Couple of months to go." He watched Morrison who seemed disoriented. Vague. Maybe unworldly was a word to describe him. He'd have to conder the description when he wrote the final draft. "Do you still write? Songs? Poetry?"

A shake of the head. A smile. "Not a word."

"Why?"

"Pointless."

"You loved music." It was a statement not a question.

Morrison pulled at his beard. Took a couple of huge breaths. Exhaled. Looked directly at Dulvey and shrugged his shoulders. "People fall out of love."

"Not just like that. Not completely."

He shrugged again. "I did."

"In Paris."

"Uh huh."

"Did something happen. Was there… an incident?"

"No," came out first. But it wasn't his real answer. He pursed his lips. Shook his head. "Maybe." He grinned. "Yes."

"What?"

Another shrug. "Long time ago. Can't really remember." He let out a long sigh. "Someone said the past is another country. For me, this is the only country. The rest… Just a dream. You know dreams. Mostly the parts don't fall into place. Don't really add up." His smile was beatific, as though he had just delivered the secret to the universe.

"Something that important, you've gotta remember,"

"Nope. Maybe the others who were there. Pammy, the doc, his niece. Cute kid, didn't say much. That guy from London."

"What guy?"

He shook his head slowly. "Music guy. I guess." He looked up into the sky, searching for shards of memory. But there was nothing left. "Friend of Pammy, maybe. Or she met him in a club." A long pause. "Or not."

Morrison had some beers cooling in the river. He retrieved a couple and they drank and smoked for a while. But nothing further of use came out.

So Mick Dulvey went to Paris. Maybe the rest of the story was there. But if it was he never wrote it.

M y dad came hoke from Costa Rica and wrote up his story so far. Then he left for Paris. And never came back.

Which is why I went to Paris. Where I tracked down just about everyone who had come into contact with Jim Morrison back in 1971. Pamela Courson was dead, the doctor who signed the death certificate was dead and just about everyone else turned out to be a dead end. Until I found the doctor's niece.

Jim was right. She had been a cute kid. She was a beautiful adult. She didn't say much because she was profoundly deaf, so her speech was difficult to understand. She avoided speaking unless she absolutely had to. It was slow going but it was not difficult to be around such a beautiful woman for a while. She introduced her self as Mireille and made him a cup of tea, serving it in China cups, sitting close to him on a sofa.

Mireille remembered everything about the night the music guy from London showed up at Morrison's flat. She spoke slowly and clearly although her vowels were elongated and some words were clipped in odd places, but her English was flawless. The Londoner was a fan boy but he figured he had an intro – a passport to Morrison's world, if even for only a brief time. Nobody introduced him to her or her uncle. She wasn't sure if even Jim knew his name

What he had was an acetate. He told Jim it was legendary in certain insider music circles in London. It had been made by a band called Chill Factor from up Newcastle way. They released two singles. The NME liked them. Made the second one single of the week. It got to number thirty-eight in the charts. Everyone (in the know) said their next one would be the one to break them. They recorded one more track, then split up. Word was the singer went back to College to study Architecture, the bassist (a boy) married the keyboard player (a girl) and they raised kids and got sensible jobs, the guitarist joined the navy and was lost at sea.

The fan boy passed the acetate to Morrison. "This is their final track. The one that was going to break them. It had a reputation as the perfect pop song. Three minutes and fifteen seconds of absolute genius. Nothing would ever better it."

Naturally Morrison was sceptical. "How come it wasn't a hit," he wanted to know.

The fan boy told him it never got to the record company. Had passed from hand to hand over a couple of years but still, somehow, never got to the right ears.

"What do you think of it?"

"Haven't played it yet," the fan boy said. An impish grin formed on mouth and travelled to his eyes. "Thought it would be better to experience with a… knowledgeable audience. Someone meaningful." He offered the disc to Morrison.

The singer made no move to accept it. His brow furrowed and he stared at the disc as though it could be boobytrapped. The fan boy, moved it towards him with an urging gesture. "Let's put it on the record deck," he said, turning abruptly and walking from the room. The fan boy followed. Mireille's uncle shrugged and indicated with a nod that they should also go along.

Morrison took the acetate and examined it carefully. "Sit, sit," he said, distractedly. Finding nothing wrong with the disc he placed it on his turntable, flipped a lever that switched the speed to forty-five, dropped the needle and took a seat himself.

Mireille watched the reactions on the faces of Morrison, her uncle and the fan boy – it was the only way she could get an indication of the quality of the music on the acetate. For the first half minute they stared at the spinning disc attentively. Then, almost as one, they sat forward in their seats, as though the volume was too low. She took out her phone and checked Google translate to find the correct word: for the second half of the record their expression was rapt. She smiled at the delivery of the word. She could tell that I appreciated her effort.

"You are not the first to ask about that night," she said. "You are a journalist also?"

I nodded. "The third?" I held up three fingers in case her lip reading of English was deficient.

She smiled and also nodded.

"What happened to them?"

"They listened to the disc. Their faces took on the same… looks? Then they left."

"The second one was my father." I typed it into my phone and showed her the screen to ensure she understood.

"He is good?"

I shook my head. "He never came home. The first journalist, the same." She read it off my phone.

Her free hand covered her mouth. She handed the phone back to me. "I'm so sorry."

I thanked her with my eyes. "Who has the disc?" I mimed a seven inch circle.

She smiled and rose from her seat gracefully, smoothing her skirt. "Come with me."

She went through a door that led to a dark hallway. There was a door on either side of the hall and another at the end. Like all the woodwork in the apartment, they were painted white. Halfway between the door on the right and the door at the end, on the wall, was a picture frame. Inside it sat the acetate. She slipped the picture frame from its hook and handed it to me. "Take it. I do not want it in the apartment any longer."

She wasn't being polite. I could see by

"People fall out of love."
"Not just like that. Not completely."

her demeanour that she genuinely wanted the acetate gone. "Thank you," I said. She kissed me on both cheeks then gave me a warm hug.

I took the acetate home. I even placed it on my turntable. But I didn't play it. I had seen for myself what it had done to Jim Morrison. I surmised that something similar had happened to Mick Dulvey and my Dad and the fan boy. It was the reason why none of them had an interest in taking the acetate when they left and seemingly had no further interest of any sort in music. I knew there was something more profound going on, else why would Jim Morrison have abandoned his life and his stardom; why would my father abandon his family as well as his career; why would Mick Dulvey disappear?

It was only in my head but the acetate seemed to radiate a sort of fatal attraction as it lay on the turntable. My eyes were drawn to it constantly. I turned my back on it and banged out my story on my laptop, then attached it to an email to my editor.

Now I feel free to proceed however I like. I have a hi-fi and I have a hammer. I am gong to use one of them. As I type this coda the hammer is definitely favourite. But I wonder if my resolve will hold if I cross the room.

Robert Neilson is a founding editor of Albedo One.

Cargo

David Murphy

I stand tall, silent as ancient oak.
You can trust me, but I'm not a tree.
I'm a derrick working hard on the deck of a ship
– a crude carrier, ocean-going bulk tanker –
reaching down, hauling up barrel by cumbersome barrel,
dark slime that glistens below the waterline.

Bill of lading unloaded, lying idle wharf-side,
I suffer a sudden crisis of conscience.
I straighten my jib, swivel the boom, withdraw all stays and pulleys,
allow sunlight burst through open hatches.

New life honeycombs the ship in an instant outbreak.
Walls of steel radicalise into molten green.
Pools of sludge transform into nascent ponds,
homes to larvae that appear in a blink from nowhere.
Flowers bloom on fragrant bulkheads.
The deck becomes awash with a meadow.

Bees tremble the massive hull with the faintest hum.
Hive-minded starlings murmurate in cool air above the ship.
When evening falls they turn onboard ladders to nesting ledges.
Moonbeams thread the hold with silver.
In the silken hour of midnight,
the captain's bridge oscillates into a *guano*-coloured cliff
alive with roosting kittiwakes.

My jib morphs into a tree – not an oak, exactly, but not far off.
Buds blossom on guys and hoists,
the living vessel beneath a floating island
riding on verdant hawsers and warps of vine.
Rocking high on waters that emit phosphorescent glows
and lap gently, no longer threatening.

Meanwhile the ship's wheel shines from the bridge,
reminding this new natural order
of the golden glow of an oil-rig at night.

David Murphy is a founding editor of Albedo One.

Cattle

Konstantine Paradias

"Betsy, you gotta put the gun down…" the words come out sounding all jumbled and wrong against the din in my ears and my nose is all backed up and thank God my throat's all tangled up in a knot so I don't throw up "…just let go, sweetheart, okay?"

Betsy makes a small, clucking noise, her beak rattling. Her clumsy, party-sausage fingers let go of the stock, but the trigger-finger's still wrapped around it, as if she's trying to somehow make it all go right back: the kick and the flash and the bang and the smell like rain pouring down the sides of a slaughterhouse.

"Paddy, get the case," I mutter. Paddy just nods, his fleece covered in red splotches, something pink and quickly drying still clinging on to it. "Paddy, come on man…"

He kneels, into the pool of sticky gunk, too numb to even shudder, reaching out with his rough, arthritic fingers, dangling out of the shaved remains of his hoof. I watch Paddy struggle with the john's grip, his fist clenched all vice-like around the briefcase handle, hear the sounds of sirens, closing in the distance.

"Help," Paddy whimpers up at me and I stomp toward him, hooves stomping into the stinking mess, turn the gun around. The barrel threatens to slip out of my grip, the palm all clammy with sweat, the fingers too long, the thumb too crooked. I bring down the butt like a hammer: once, twice. Something snaps inside the gun and the magazine comes spilling out. Paddy tries to grab at it, but ends up spilling a half-dozen bullets all over the floor.

"Leave them. Paddy, leave them!" I hiss at him and Paddy stops, halfway through stuffing the gunk-crusted bullets in his pockets, tries to stand up, kneels down, grabs the case, wraps his fore-legs around it like it's a baby. Betsy's already up on her feet, her wing looking like it's busted, all bent out of shape. Still, she hobbles right up behind us, clucking real gently and hands me the keys.

"Butch, do you mind?" she whispers, softly and hops into the backseat, still shuddering. I just open the driver's seat and start taking out the high-chair, the pedal-assist, even rip out the back of the seat, just to I'd get some space. Even after all this, I still have to bend my knees so far back they all but touch my chest. I cringe, as my filed horn tip drags against the faux-leather roof. From the rear-view mirror, I check Paddy's thousand-yard stare, catch Betsie tugging at a stray feather sticking out of her busted wing and I lie:

"It's all gonna be worth it. Every last bit."

HANDS GOOD. SPINE STRAIGHT.

The reel rolls across the cafeteria walls, the subway glass panes; it plays out in between ad breaks of zooperas and in the wee hours before dawn.

THUMBS TO WORK AND MAKE US GREAT!

Human hands, swathed in plastic film, straightening spines and adding parts to brains; rows on rows on rows of hands, grafted in the place where hooves used to be.

EYES FRONT, THINK HARD.

Filed horns and brand new eyes fitted for new skulls and clothes, grafted onto hides to mask the thick smell of pelt and fleece, the feel of bristling curls and the *trod trod trod* of hindlegs and webbed feet and the clatter of claws.

WORK, BE FREE AND JOIN THE FARM!

Cut to black. A moment of silence. Distant trill of violins as the rosy glow of dawn comes and the world fades into green pasture and mountains of hay and a ruby red barn, all animal sounds coming from inside, a toneless cacophony that brings a tear to your eye.

And the image becomes a still that lingers on the screen, gets burned into your brain deeper than any brand and it hurts worse than the graft-aches, burns worse than any of the food allergies, itches more than any phantom limb.

And the more you want it, the faster it kills you.

"Heard the news?" Betsy clucks at me as I'm wheeling the produce dolly, peeking her head out from the edge of the cubicle. On her high chair, the memory foam practice egg she's been trying to peddle as her own since forever begins to swell back into its too-perfect shape "they're sending Donny out to the Farm!"

"No way," Paddy says, his head sticking out like a wad of cotton candy, white and virginal, almost model material.

"Ain't that a shame," I say, easing the dolly down slow, looking to all the world like I'm taking a breather. "Only goat in Accounting that could hold a conversation and he's about to go away forever."

"Word round the trough is, he's going all the way," Betsy says, leaning her head down so low, that her finely arranged comb drapes down one eye "Full conversion."

Hands good. Spine straight. Thumbs to work and make us great!

"Well I'll be damned; ol' Donny the square's going barnyard," Paddy chuckles a little too loud, eyes darting out to the roving drone-cam that buzzes over our heads. "I just hope the feed's worth it."

The drone-cam hovers over us, pivots, then slowly turns, taking us in, the single bird-eye hidden behind its lens blinking a hundred times a second. Betsy clucks before she knows she's done it and the drone-cam snaps around, its lens extending toward her, eye blinking *click-click-click-click-click* and Betsy looks about ready to have a fit, her pudgy little hands at the end of her wings clenched so tight they look almost bone-white at the knuckle. I see her throat wobble and her beak rattle and I *know* she's about to cluck again and that some human up in Control's going to dock her for it so I talk before I've even thought about it.

"Dolly wheel's wonky. Doing a check," I tell the drone-cam. In a split-second, it's pulled away from Betsy, snapping back at me, elevating until it's on eye level. From its side, a beam of light shoots out, reading the code imprinted on my ear. There's a beep, a series of humming noises and a strip of printed paper comes out the front and drifts to the floor. The drone-cam lets out a string of nonsense from its built-in headphone and then zips away, to ruin someone else's day.

"Butch, what did you *do*, man?" Paddy says, staring out at the tiny metal ball, bobbing and weaving across the cubicles, sprinkling its printed slips as it goes.

"Don't speak Man, man. I'm Storage," I shrug and pick up the slip. There's just three words written down there but they're enough to drag the world out from under me:

WORKPLACE LOITERING -50%

"Oh Butch, I'm..." Betsy clucks but I don't have the time to stick around. Little slip's just cut my rent and grub by half and it means at least 40 more hours down in the dark, moving crates unless I'm looking to spend 3 more years, lugging around produce before my back finally gives out.

"It's okay," I mutter.

"Catch you lunchtime?" Paddy calls out as I'm rolling the dolly into the merchandise elevator all the way down to Logistics Hell and I just nod and smile but we both know he doesn't really mean it.

The back streets snake across town, all the way to the electrified fencing at the edge of the Reptile Exclusion Zone. From the corner of my eye, I can see Paddy leaning against the passenger side window, his head trailing the giant ferns that brush across the side of the car.

"I'm sorry. I slipped," Betsy says and we simply sit there in the car for a quiet eternity, listening to the sound the ferns make across the brushed chassis, taking in the smell of leather and offal and gunpowder and fear.

"We had him! Goddamn it Betsy, we had the old fart," Paddy says, slamming his hand against the dashboard, roaring "we were out of there; out, out, out!"

"I told you, I'm..." Betsy starts, but Paddy just leans back, starts kicking like a kid at the empty air, smashes the glove compartment padlock, tears at his perfect intact tufts of wool.

"Jeez Paddy, will you just shut up," I say and Paddy stops, staring at me as if I just walked in brandishing a butcher knife "it's done, okay? We did it and we're running and when they're done sweeping the place we'll be as good as caught."

The words come out all at once, without a hint of hesitation or fear; there's not all that much to mull over, when you really look at it. Looking back, we were all doomed the second we decided to go with Paddy's nonsense.

"I can't go. I can't go, I was close! I was so damn close..." Paddy's words trail into a long, winding bleat and I pull the car over, by the ruins of the Old Town precinct, now choked by monster vines and gigantic magnolias, blooming under the moonlight.

In the distance, something lets out a roar that sounds a lot like the scream of a woman.

"Butch, what are you doing?" Betsy says and my thumbs trace the handle of the gun, handing off the leather strap near my waistband, then I say:

"We need a fall guy."

"Paddy's gone packing," Betsy says, leaning over in her high chair. On stage, a man from Contol, covered in creaking hard plastic from head to toe, is letting out a string of gibberish while some schmaltzy slideshow plays in the background.

"What?" I mutter right back at her, keeping an eye out at the stage, at Donny, his blown glass lifetime achievement award in his gnarled, hairy man-hands, his wrinkled accountant's suit stapled to his hide, looking bored out of his skull.

"Control caught him moonlighting. Went against his Production contract, so they had him out the door in fifteen minutes," Betsy whispers, her voice rising in pitch, turning into a tiny, hen-like whine. From across the auditorium, a Mangalitza from QA *shushes* her.

"It's fine. Paddy can do it. He's a smart trotter. Smarter than me," I say and the man from Control steps back from the podium, letting Donny trot his way behind the mic. The old goat just stands there for a while, licking his lips, letting his long tongue wrap around his mouth, clatters his teeth, then goes:

"Sorry, I was just practicing my Barnyard. How did I do?"

And right on cue, the audience explodes into laughter. Betsy does it too, a short little howl, just for show, just as the first wave of drone-cams begins to sweep across the auditorium.

"Paddy said he wants to talk," Betsy says, while the laughter and the clapping are still going, low enough so it gets lost in the hubbub. "Says he's got it figured out."

"Tell Paddy he's better off calming down and looking for any place that can take him," I mutter back, just as a group of mules from HR begin to wheel in a cardboard cutout stage from the Farm and a chorus of Accounting goats begin to bleat and trot around Donny, looking sad and angry all at once, "and you best pipe down too. You're gonna have a clutch of chicks to take care off before you know it."

"I'm egg-bound, Butch," Betsy says, just as the laughter and the chorus dies down. On stage, Donny takes a bow and the man in the plastic wrap starts to mumble nonsense, while we all start to file down the room. In my chest, a great big hand, as cold as winter, wraps itself around my heart and *squeezes*.

"Six o'clock. Archiving. Show up if you're gonna," Betsy says and I watch her slip past the crowd with the rest of the poultry.

Two hours later, I'm halfway through stacking crates in 7G, when the world fades away from me and I find myself laying on the concrete floor, legs kicking against my will. A passing drone-cam passes by me and snaps a shot of me as I'm screaming.

When I come to, I see it: my mouth hanging open, my eyes rolled to the back of my head and I think I'm not looking too bad, dead.

"You're not taking my goddamn money," Donny the goat says, his sideways slitted eyes taking all of us in; the black spray on our clothes, the crude balaclava masks, the jittery handgun that Paddy lifted off Terminations, "and I wanna know: who gives a hen a damn gun?"

"Shut *aaahhh*," Paddy says, the words trailing into a bleat, then finally manages, "Shut up."

"I bet it was your idea, wasn't it, you little wether?" Donny says and Paddy lashes out at him before I've had a chance to stop him, foreleg flailing out. Donny's head snaps back and when he turns, I can see the swelling growing in one eye.

"Pipe down now..." I say, the voice toned down in a low, rumbling tone but that just makes Donny break into a laugh that turns into a high-pitched, evil-sounding cackle.

"You know, I didn't want to go to the Farm? What good is it, getting your hands cut off and your back broken, just

so you can fit in?" Donny says, staring up at me, his eyes trailing across my forelegs, my legs, my hands, probably weighing his options.

"The money, Donny..." I tell the goat, reaching out my hand to squeeze his shoulder, giving him a taste. Some of the spunk seems to drain away from him all of a sudden. It's not much, but it's enough to make a difference.

"I told them and I told them. I begged, even; you ever seen a billy goat begging? Saddest sight you'll see," Donny said as he left his chair, headed for the bedroom, the three of us trailing behind him "but you know what they told me, after thirteen years of service?"

Eyes fixed on the goat, we watch him trace a secret pathway on the floor. Running across the hardwood, the tips of his fingers find a latch, grab on and then *pull* and just like that, a patch of floor recedes into darkness.

"'Don't you worry Donny my boy; when the boys pull out those cortical implants, you won't even remember you were ever here'," Donny says, twisting his mouth to give his voice that human drawl that haunts every TV set, pours out of every speaker. "Now what the hell kind of answer is that?"

Jimmying his hand into the opening, the goat pulls out his briefcase, covered in dust and locked up tight, its casing a muted gunmetal grey. Paddy leans in to grab it, hand reaching for the handle, when Donny's horns smash into his skull and send him flying.

"You ain't getting my money," Donny says and charges at me, horns down. I reach out my hands to grab him, put every ounce of strength I've got but he still hits me with enough force to drive me through the closet door and knock the wind out of my lungs.

Donny raises his hoof and stomps my chest once, twice, before Paddy grabs him by the ankle and twists. The old goat tries to pull away but Paddy shoots up onto his knees, slams him down on the floor. They're rolling down on the hardwood, bleating at each other and I'm up on my feet, reaching for the case, when Betsy's finger slips.

There's a sound like thunder breaking out in a teacup, replaced by a deep and piercing din. There's a patch of red over my eye and, somewhere far away, the sound of a tiny voice weeping.

"Betsy, you gotta put the gun down..."

Betsy volunteers before we've even drawn straws, but I go through it anyway: we use magnolia anthers to pick which one of us will go up to the screaming sirens, gun in hand and give himself up so the rest can go.

I've been told it's a very human thing to do, but I wouldn't know, really.

"Betsy said..." Paddy begins but I just give him a long, hard stare until he's stopped fidgeting and the anthers in the lams of my hands, all nice and mixed up. I hand first pick to Betsy and she reaches for them with her one good hand, the other slowly turning swollen and purple.

She draws it away from my grip, a long, thin and perfect piece and I can hear myself and Paddy groan in tandem. Betsy makes a series of soft, sucking noises and it takes me some time to realize that she's crying.

Paddy goes next, his fingers tracing the anther tips, testing the pollen clinging to the tips of his fingers as if searching for a sign then slowly languidly pulls at his pick. We hold our breath as the strand comes out, then suddenly tapers off, dangling from the tip of his fingers.

"No," Paddy moans and I grab him by the shoulders and pull him in, even as he pushes against me and moans into my suit "no, no, damnit no!"

"I can go..." Betsy begins but I shush her. In the distance, the lone trills of sirens becomes a chorus, drawing ever closer.

"It wasn't gonna go that way Butch, I swear..."

"I know."

"Don't make me go, Butch, don't make me go..."

"I'll stick with you, okay?" I tell Paddy and he bleats, a tiny, moaning noise and nods "until we get there."

I wait for Paddy to pipe down and we make the switch, him on the driver's side and me sitting shotgun, the gun laid out on the dashboard between us. Betsy lingers at the door for a while, then jumps to the curb and watches us go. If I didn't know any better, I'd say she's happy to be left out of it, dead hen walking or not.

We're halfway to downtown, headed toward the shimmering ring of cop car lights, when Paddy says:

"You think they'll make it quick?"

"Quicker than what we'd get if they had to catch us," I say but I know that I'm not helping. "Are you sure you can do this?"

"I pulled the short end, didn't I?" Paddy hisses at me and pulls over, stuffing the gun in his jacket pocket. "You'd better leg it. It's going to look better if I've stolen the ride."

I nod and linger by the passenger side, watching Paddy as he trots over to the street, hands raised up in the air, calling out his man nonsense just as I make the turn. In the distance, there's a stream of jabber, augmented from a megaphone. Without thinking, I take the two short anthers from my pocket and stick them in my mouth, swallow without even bothering to chew.

From somewhere far away, there's the rumble of thunder, but no rain.

Konstantine Paradias is a writer by choice.

His work has been featured in magazines and videogames like Raft, Scrap Mechanic and Flintlock: the Siege of Dawn, but is most proud to be part of this iconic speculative fiction magazine. He wishes you, the reader, the endurance and wisdom to make the most out of rejection and the strength and courage to achieve your dreams.

The Nape of Marie Antoinette

—a further voyage of the Chinese Time Machine

Ian Watson

フランスで最も美しい王妃
マリ・アントワネットに栄光あれ

"I'll be demmed!"

Sir Percy drawls this oath in a lazy foppish way. Yet his blue eyes are piercingly intent upon the visitor to his flat in Paris's normally fashionable Rue de Richelieu – though down any alleyway you'll encounter the original medieval warren, dingy, dirty.

Most men who pass by outside wear tatty red bonnets and tricoleur cockades. Striped or plain trousers have replaced bourgeois breeches sporting knee buckles. Women wear full swirling peasant skirts, forever a mob in the making. Carts carry heaps of headless chickens, horse hoofs for glue, barrels of wine. When in public, it's wise to call this Rue by its new revolutionary name *Law Street*.

The mysterious stranger is dark-clad. His almondy eyes lack folds. Maybe a Chinaman?

"You say you come from how many years ahead – ?"

"Two hundred and sixty years, Lord Blakeney."

Sir Percy Blakeney utters a short sheeplike laugh at the oriental fellow's error of etiquette – for a baronet most certainly isn't a lord. He lets this faux-pas pass; the credential of the eastern fella is persuasive.

Namely, an oversize visiting card. On the blank side, the word POSTCARD, a word new to Sir Percy although self-explanatory. On the glossy front is a view claiming to be "Richmond", which is where Sir Percy has his magnificent mansion house within private grounds.

Richmond Bridge – and Eel Pie Island beyond in the Thames – are readily recognizable... Yet whence that township just south of the Thames? How has the hamlet of Richmond mushroomed so much?

The viewpoint is as if the summit of Richmond Hill has come much closer to Richmond Bridge than in reality. As if one of those new-fangled de Montgolfier aerostat globes affords a platform up in the air. Sir Percy sees clearly all the way to Twittenham where Pope the poet lived till fifty years previously. Yet the view is so sharply precise. Not painted, nor engraved. More like a tiny window – upon another realm of reality, at once familiar yet uncannily alien.

Dammit but the central arch of the five-span stone bridge has visibly been *lowered*; it's less humpbacked than Percy remembers it being, to allow biggish boats to pass underneath. However, contrariwise and nonsensically, the Thames rises higher up the arches than Sir Percy has ever seen, flooding out beyond its usual banks. Of Eel Pie Island there's surely less land.

"What's wrong with the Thames?" Percy drawls at the oriental fella.

"The world's ice is melting," Tanaka answers indifferently. Japan is a tall country mostly.

"Be demmed."

"In my time your rescues of French nobles from the Reign of Terror are inscribed in history, Lord Blakeney – "

"What's all this to me? I'm Sir Percy. Or Mi'Lord. Never 'Lord Blakeney'."

"*Sumimasen, Dannasama.* Consequently I happen to know the exact date of the Queen's trial, *which isn't any day soon*, followed next day by her execution by guillotine at exactly half past noon – "

"So, an exact execution." As a fop when in public, Sir Percy is given to witticisms.

"Gadzooks. The exact date, pray?"

"I've no intention of concealing the date from you as bait, Sir Percy, but – " The oriental chap nods significantly in the direction of young Sir Andrew Ffoulkes sprawled along the sheep-bone sofa, negligently intent upon their conversation.

"Lud, man, you may speak in front of this honoured guest of mine."

So Tanaka continues, "I do realise how you and your friends need ample time to lay plans for safety, also for surprise. I can assure you that I am no tool of Citizen Chauvelin, if you might suspect so."

At the mention of Sir Percy's adversary, Sir Andrew erupts like a game bird flushed from cover. Already he's tugging the brocade curtains of the nearest window shut. "Beware, Sir, for your life may be forfeit."

"Bah," retorts the oriental.

Willing to continue his masquerade to see what more he may learn, Sir Percy adjusts his costly lace cuffs, teases from his waistcoat a tiny silver snuff box, and helps himself to a pinch.

"Citizen... what? *Chauve-souris* did you say?"

Komori, murmurs an uptime high-tech lingo collar. *Bat*.

The visitor gazes steadily at Sir Percy. Again, that rustle of whispered words as if moths beat wings within the oriental's shirt up near his collar. "A *chauve-souris* may be impossible to spot on a dark night. They seek it here, they seek it there, those Frenchies seek it everywhere, that demmed elusive Pimpernel. Your own words, I believe, Sir Percy *secretly the Pimpernel*."

Tanaka knows that despite Sir Percy being built like a bull he himself can easily kill the Englishman if need be using the short wakizashi hidden under his tunic. Gods forbid any such thing shall happen! *Kami wa kinjinasai!* Tanaka long admired this English ninja of eighteen eras before his own time, due to the Englishman's supreme skill at deception and disguise which lets Sir Percy Blakeney carry out seemingly impossible rescues and escapes.

Courtesy of a Chinese time machine hijacked by wielding the same wakizashi, here they are now together in this drawing room, and Tanaka can offer Sir Percy the perfect *challenge*, of rescuing Queen Marie Antoinette herself from the very scaffold of the guillotine itself. Smoke and mirrors, monomolecular mirrors-cloak! At least until the final moment, the moment which will bring Tanaka's career to a climax. His libidinal career.

Built like a bull, Sir Percy, indeed. A massive man, unusually tall and broad-shouldered. Breeches close-fitting as can be over sculptural legs. On a whim Sir Percy famously put up fists against Red Sam and thoroughly bested that brick wall of a pugilist.

Yet well-attested tales tell of the Pimpernel disguising himself successfully as a stooping old crone, or a squat washer-woman, or a slinking Jewish pedlar. Another time, as a grimacing fishwife carrying a brawny baby. *How is this accomplished?*

Sir Percy's parents love each other deeply. Their first two years of married bliss culminate in the birth of Percy, fully nine pounds when he pops out. Dizzy with delight, the young mother scorns the services of any wet nurses and takes baby Percy to bed with herself to suckle. Devotedly indulgent dad Sir Algernon is perfectly amenable to this arrangement, so long as it doesn't continue beyond a month or two...

Lady Blakeney – as was – awakes to moonlight streaming in to her bedchamber. Her silk sheet has slipped down, as has her lacy nightgown from her shoulders.

Suckling at her left breast is hungry small baby Percy. Sucking from her right breast also is thirsty little Percy. At both breasts, twin babes. Or one and the same babe twice.

Lady Blakeney's screams echo through the corridors of the riverside mansion at Richmond.

Sir Algernon arrives from his own bedchamber within moments, followed by two dishevelled flunkeys bearing candles who gape at their lady bare-tits in bed by the light of Luna. Lady Blakeney's own chambermaid rushes in *en déshabillé*.

"What's wrong, my Love, what's wrong? Did our bouncy boy bite you?"

If only that were so.

At Lady Blakeney's left tit, burly baby Percy, only son so far, is wriggling like some snake swiftly swallowing another snake which itself is swallowing the outer snake from within.

From that moment onward Sir Algernon's lovely young wife becomes a lunatic. Lightly lunatic to begin with; she can still converse, just not about their son. Soon she beholds other things which a human mind rejects. Such as two short squat toddlers playing hide and seek before tumbling over one another and merging. Somehow clothing conforms. And Lady B becomes more deeply imbecile.

She's only suited to hide abroad in a little palace in Portugal, along with nursemaids, a cook, and a flunkey or two – presently adding tutors to educate the child in etiquette, fencing, French, accountancy since he's sole heir to vast wealth; that mad wife will bear no other child.

Sir Algy's son forever sympathises with aristocrats after he returns to his homeland, by now a strapping young fella, fashionable and frivolous. This and his vast ballast of wealth may stabilise him, keep him normal. However, here comes the French Revolution which in due course brings the Guillotine which industrialises the beheadings of nobles... as well as of cartloads of ignobles and of innocents such as exploited whores.

The hijack of the Time Machine from Oxford 2052 takes Colonel Maggie Mo by such surprise.

She's in the banqueting hall of Oxford's Randolph Hotel repurposed to house the time machine called the Pod, product of Beijing's Time Institute. She's with her two tame Brit Dons, Sharma (19th century Eng Lit) and Mason (History of Ideas), useful chaps for time jaunts up to date. In view of what's to come it's fortunate that our academics are wearing regular jackets and cords today, not flamboyant British officer's uniforms such as when they went along with Maggie to 1815 St Helena, enough said about which for the mo.

Prior to this confab with Maggie at the Randolph the pair breakfasted at

Toffs in Oxford's Covered Market. Their bill for Eggs Benedict with snifters of Cognac is refunded promptly by one of Maggie's staff since this is official secret business. *Namely*, about uptime China maybe assisting compassionately, secretly, and cunningly the Irish during the mid-19th century potato famine, which may have political consequences as regards the Kennedy clan (and even the number of Irish in the NYPD).

For this purpose a pair of Brits masquerading as overlords will once again be potent puppets. Dusky Sharma will pretend to be a Protestant Hindu Indian prince serving the British Empire, a Baba or Raja or Nawab or something. Nuances, yet to be polished. Noodles and rice shall become the staple diet for the Irish. Bogs will be paddy fields for cold climate cultivars. Where and *when* exactly should China intervene?

A pair of Maggie's Guoanbu security gals in their smart blue tailored suits are vigilant near the doors – when suddenly it's as if the intruder drops from the ceiling. He's in some gossamer chameleon or octopus smartcloak that can only be NipponTech. Becoming more visible, with his left hand he seizes Maggie's collar tightly. His right hand is brandishing a short wakizashi, its blade bright, held well aside as yet from both of their bodies.

The Guoanbu gals can't do much with their pock-pock pistols without peppering Maggie. As they nevertheless circle quickly closer, their knives can be no match for a wakizashi whack.

"Nobody move!" the intruder shouts in very acceptable Mandarin. Sad to say, NipTech lingo collars are slightly superior to lingo collars made in China.

What Maggie doesn't do is any of her Krav Maga high jinks. Instead, with one foot she boots David Mason, History of Ideas, in the tweed-clad bum, propelling him at the Pod's open hatch while shrieking at Sharma, "Rajit! Get Mason and yourself inside, brace, and lie low!"

That's gratifyingly protective of her. Also, Maggie's piercing shriek disorients her assailant. Or maybe there's recoil from her kick. But she could swear that her captor softly *licks her neck*. This is so unexpected that for a mo she loses initiative while she analyses. That's enough for the samurai or ninja, whatever his fantasy, to swing Maggie at the pod – into which he throws her sprawling. Wakizashi to the fore, he follows swiftly. Hatch latches. Moments later the security duo are at the porthole of the hatch, prying and scratching, all in vain.

"Go *now* immediately to 1793 Paris 4 October. Near the city centre. Or I hurt one gaijin, gwailo."

"Gwailo foreigner Gaijin outsider," pipes up one of the Chinese lingo collars lying by the controls, switching on of its own accord like a pesky Alexa.

"But why, Son of the Rising Sun-san?" Maggie temporises. "And what time of day or night?"

"I say," says Prof Mason, unhappy at any delay while a whacky zashi is in an unpredictable hand, as he understands.

"I think the French King was guillotined *early* in 1793," says Sharma. "But as for *October* – "

Maggie replies reasonably, "I can check up on my HandyHan. Half a tick."

"**No delay!** Pre-dawn may be best. *Now*! Neck *kubi* neck *kubi*," the fellow jabbers. "Unagi, freshwater eel? No, *Unaji* is the *nape, la nuque*."

Their would-be hijacker may be unhinged rather than being an agent of the Japanese state. A deranged fanatic, an insane-san.

The stranger reaches forward swiftly and pricks Mason who squeals.

"I said now!"

So Maggie obliges.

"May we know your name, Mister - san?"

"How long till we arrive in Paris? Quickly! Vite!"

It seems the hijacker has little direct familiarity with operating a time machine although he certainly knows where to locate the world's prototype in Oxford in 2052.

"I am Tanaka Toshi," shouts their abductor.

"Excuse me." Maggie consults her top-of-the-range HandyHan fount of info. The smartphone carries a chipshop full of facts internally even if there's no coverage to reach any info cloud within centuries of itself.

"Are you by any chance the prosperous publisher of the Japanese fetish magazine *Blood on Blades*? Also of the bondage monthly, *Knots and Limbs*? Not to mention *Nude Necks over Knees?*"

"C'est vrai. So what! **How long?**"

"We shall arrive in Paris 1793 in about eight minutes, Tanaka-san. And 239 years ago. If that isn't too long to hold your *tanto* tight."

"Yes, you may refer to my sword as a *tanto* as well as *wakizashi*. Respect." This is like reverse-Stockholm gambit being played out.

Calmly, "So why do you wish to be in the bloodiest midst of the French Revolution?"

Red-faced, Toshio Tanaka sucks in his breath. "Because."

"There's always cause, Tanaka-san, unless you're hopelessly mad. I see that you love blades. You wish to behold the guillotine at its busiest? I wonder does anyone special get the chop on the 4th or 5th of October...? Hmm, how exactly do you plan to get back home afterwards? – or *doesn't that matter*? Not if you can use your camo cloak and your ninja skill... to rescue somebody with filthy rich connections?"

> "What's wrong with the Thames?" Percy drawls at the oriental fella. "The world's ice is melting," Tanaka answers indifferently. Japan is a tall country mostly.

"Just you mind your own business."

"30 seconds to destination plus or minus 10," from Rajit Sharma.

"HandyHan: French Revolution, who's the most important guillotined celebrity from October 1793 query."

The ceramic Pod shudders to a stop amidst grey trees and bushes visible through the porthole in pre-dawn light. Roosting pigeons take wing, pushed by expanding air.

"*Marie Antoinette ex-Queen of France.*"

Already Toshio Tanaka has the hatch open and leaps out, wakizashi wagging as his rearguard.

"You're here to save Marie Antoinette from the guillotine! Don't be crazy!"

Tanaka rushes away, a swirl lost amidst shadows. Maggie Mo darts after

A deranged fanatic, an insane-san.

him for a short way. Already the man has disappeared – as well might anybody amidst the tangle of shrubbery beneath, yes, pear trees – some rotten fruit underfoot says so, squelch, though less than you might expect in such a neglected orchard, rats must enjoy pears.

On returning to the hatch, "Our kidnapper's gone."

"So now the three of us can go home," rejoices Mason from within the Pod.

"Not likely!" while Sharma emerges. "If by using some 2050s tech Ninja Tanaka manages to spirit Marie Antoinette to safety, there must be significant upsets. Invasion by Austria, Russia... Who knows, maybe no Napoleonic Empire!"

"So where will us three have been to in 1815, you mean? *Harrumph.*"

Sharma has never actually heard anyone say *harrumph* before.

Maggie Mo quickly asks, "HandyHan, what day does the ex-Queen die?"

"*October 16th.*"

From Maggie, "Tanaka is giving himself twelve days to recce and prepare. Obviously he can't have any collaborators as yet. He must be carrying diamonds for living expenses, bribes. Gold weighs you down. What was the paper currency pre-Napoleon – ?"

"*Assignats,*" supplies Sharma, forever intent on being helpful. Assy-Nyats. "The legal paper currency of the revolution, seeing as the coffers of the French Treasury are empty. High-value ones are easy to print if you're a publisher."

"Any forger of assignats is for the chop sharpish. Nobody in their right mind should take the risk. Though who can be in their right mind in Paris right now?"

Distant cocks crow and church bells cling as dawn strengthens towards day, revealing a neglected jungle of orchard fringing a vast misty expanse of tree-lined formal gardens.

"Where are we?" Maggie demands of Sharma. "Versailles?"

"Not likely. Versailles palace is abandoned. The Queen's in prison. I'm sure I've been here, Colonel Mo, up-time. I think, I think these are the Luxembourg Gardens."

Maggie nods. "HandyHan, map of Paris 1793, tag Luxembourg Gardens, display route to China Consul."

"But," protests Prof Mason, "there can't possibly be Chinese diplomats here so soon!"

As if to shame Mason, HandyHan pipes up, "*Choses Chinoises, Quai d'Orfèvres, Île de la Cité.*"

"Stuff From China, Goldsmiths Quay, City Island," says a lingo collar.

"Looks quite close," from Maggie.

"But how how *how?*" from Mason.

"Waste of time telling you till I confirm. Take off those posh jackets, rub them on their ground a bit to dirty them. My uniform can pass as the livery of some cancelled aristo."

Since it's still only after eight in the morning and there's no quarry in sight, Maggie sets an easy pace. The Pod should stay safely hidden in its unseeable shimmer mode inside the overgrown orchard. HandyHan says that Napoleon will order the orchard to be tidied as part of urban improvements once he's emperor. First, he'll need to sort out the map of Europe.

'City Island' houses at one end the cathedral of Notre Dame and at the other end the Law Courts surrounded by swanky shops. Up top is the huge Concièrgerie palace sitting upon a multitude of damp dingy dungeons where condemned prisoners await transport by cart to the guillotine, a prolonged ride of shame away. Extraordinarily Marie Antoinette has been held underneath the Concièrgerie for weeks of misery instead of the usual two or three days.

Boats ply the river. Smart shops offer de luxe perfumes, umbrellas and walking canes, fans and bow ties, exquisite stationery, leather boots.

"Queen's an incestuous cunt!" bellows a crier, squinting at a printed sheet.

"I say," says Mason, "that's a bit stiff."

From Sharma, "That bit of slander's probably being paid for by the Jacobites, I mean Jacobins."

Irrespective of beggars, shrill harridans, foul-mouthed town criers, soldiers in uniform toting muskets, gendarmes with sabres, proles and peasants sporting their tricoleurs, there's a lot of elegance and politeness too, at least hereabouts. A posh ladies hairdresser is still essaying reduced versions of the puffy bouffant style which became a craze due to Marie Antoinette. Pre-revolution, ladies of quality gladly knelt on the floors of their carriages to protect their ever-higher hairpieces from being bumped. Nowadays so much ostentation invites a trip to the guillotine, but hair-dressing necessarily continues. Next door to the ladies hairdresser, a smart café offers coffees and chocolates. Alas, our three lack money for the moment.

Thus they arrive at *Choses Chinoises*, its window displaying blue and white vases, sheet wallpaper of golden pheasants or red and white carp, cinnabar lacquerware, jade figurines, painted fans.

Within they find an oriental man of late middle age who wears a yellow cape over a robe decorated with dragons. A long pigtail is tied by an exemplary tricoleur silken bow.

"Citizens, you honour my establishment." Mason and Sharma in their soiled worsted jackets pass without much scrutiny, but the proprietor certainly heeds Maggie in her Chinese Communist Party Security Service uniform. From an inner pocket Maggie produces a slim seal-stamp carved from milky green jade, which she shows to the shopkeeper. A novelty to the Oxonians.

"*Chuán guó xǐ!*" gasps the man. Tears start to his eyes. "An Heirloom Seal of the Realm... I never thought... I thought these are legend... that none survives... Will you permit me to touch it?"

Maggie Mo smiles. "I even permit you to *print* with it – upon a receipt for the assignats which I must urgently request from you for a mission. By the imprint you shall know that your loan is guaranteed down the ages by the Mandate of Heaven."

"Yes yes, I understand it is so. My privilege is enormous. You are an agent of the eternal state."

"You are its attentive ears in France, and its nimble fingers if need be."

"Small need in the near future, I'd say. My ears hear that the Qianlong Emperor rejects the crude trade goods and clumsy diplomacy of the brutish British Kingdom. Likewise of the Franks who savagely decapitate a monarch. I can safely confide in you, Great Lady of the Mandate."

"You do well to confide. On this very topic of decapitation we will greatly value your best information about Queen Marie Antoinette who yet remains alive – "

Green tea with date-cakes is taken privately in Bingwen Bi's office, for such is the Chinoiserie factor's name. Appropriately that signifies 'Jade Connoiseur.' Sort of. After serving refreshments, Bingwen Bi's adequately buxom daughter Baozhai, Precious Hairpin, sets out to find outer garb to replace Mason's and Sharma's bourgeois jackets. Maggie Mo is already relaxing in a well-used padded coat embroidered with faded orchids, to hide her odd uniform.

Mason strives to control his desire for another date-cake. Hell, it's only a couple of hours since the two dons breakfasted.

Bingwen Bi frowns. "The filthy River Seine running past the Concièrgerie prison ensures that cells are always damp and mouldy. It seems that the queen is in such a cell under close and permanent observation by coarse guards stationed within the very cell itself. A token screen provides scant privacy. The guards may watch the Queen use the potty any time they please. They foul the damp air by smoking. They bellow curses while they play piquet drunkenly. The whole labyrinth of dungeons is a bedlam of noise and disease. Vicious guard dogs bark and bite. Almost every possession has been confiscated from the Queen by now – including her children. Her clothes are ragging and rotting yet she mends them patiently. All day she can only sit, and seemingly pray to the God of Catholics. She haemorrhages from her womb. Thus it has been for Marie Antoinette since the start of August, two vile and wretched months – whereas other inmates only languish in the Concièrgerie two days for trial and sentencing followed a few hours later by execution."

"I say," says Mason, "she must be resilient."

The Chinese factor resumes. "Marie Antoinette is only 36 years old yet near the end of her tether physically. Despite a hundred humiliations she is polite and gracious – and she is concerned not to risk the safety of other people who support her and who make plans to rescue her – all of which plans so far fail, due to police spies or due to sheer chance, feeding more victims to the guillotine."

"I always thought of her as being a sort of brainless blonde bombshell – "

" – strawberry blonde, actually," says Sharma.

" – who bankrupted France by her extravagance."

"She is so accused," confirms the Chinoiserie factor, "and she was vastly frivolous while the Court was at Versailles, yet now she has the mettle of a man more than her vacillating royal husband ever had. Her hair is pitiable. Incidentally, she introduced a special high pouf hair styled to popularise vaccination against smallpox. Not wholly an airhead, Marie Antoinette. Her cheeks are sunken now. Her legs swell painfully. So I hear."

"You hear very well," Maggie compliments Bingwen Bi. "What an excellent agent you are for our Central Kingdom."

"If I might presume to hear some more, this trio may also attempt to rescue the Queen?"

Maggie's hand cuts the air for silence from Mason and Sharma, no indiscretions guys. When Maggie concentrates intensely, she can have the aspect of a praying as well as a preying mantis about to seize an insect by the neck to suck its juices.

"Bingwen Bi, I would appreciate your assistance in renting a place to stay. Bedrooms to consist of one for myself, one for these two men. No bedbugs, lice, fleas, ticks. Rats only in the walls. Location, on the route between the Concièrgerie and the site of the guillotine."

"La Place de la Révolution," supplies the Chinaman, "formerly Place Louis Quinze."

"I say – " says Mason.

"No, you do not say," says Maggie.

"Excuse me," from Bingwen Bi discreetly. "I must fetch money." Ah, the money isn't kept in the office; that's sage of him. He withdraws.

Sharply, "We will *not* go near to the Pod until our mission is clear. We'll live wherever seems most convenient regarding Tanaka's motives and abilities. If the Pod is noticed and breached and damaged, we shall not be neutralised along with it."

From Mason, "Do you reckon Bingo hears what he hears from a gang of paid street urchins resembling the Baker Street Irregulars?"

"Maybe so. But he has to protect his sources. I shouldn't ask."

"If something goes askew and we're obliged to travel forward through time the normal day-by-day way, may we meet up with our own selves on St Helena 20-ish years from now?" As the younger don, Sharma likely has more years ahead of him in case of such a sabbatical. "Meanwhile we'll have access to a ready cash box."

"Rajit oh Rajit, we mustn't even think of abusing an Imperial Heirloom Seal of the Realm. The copies of the seal were initiated by the very first ruler of a unified China – Qin Shi Yuang himself of the Terracotta Army – to be handed down *irrespective* of whichever dynastic house rules to assist regarding unguessable future contingencies that could face the Chinese Empire. That could even include creatures coming from outer space."

"Sorry. Very foresightful."

"Celestial oversight of China, Rajit." But then she winks.

Soon Bingwen Bi returns with a fat bundle of printed assignats. "Lady of the Mandate, the value of these will surely plummet if not used. Five billion are in circulation."

"Can you let it be known that somebody is very interested in the whereabouts of a newly-arrived oriental man about 50 years old but very nimble who is obsessed with Marie Antoinette."

Bingwen Bi inclines his head. "That description certainly narrows the field amongst orientals strolling the streets."

"100 livres reward to the informant."

Graciously, "Which you are now readily able to pay, Lady of the Mandate. May I suggest an assignat worth 10 livres, otherwise you draw too much attention? Police spies are everywhere."

Maggie nods. "*Obsessed*, I repeat, but in *what way* exactly? For what purpose?"

"To rescue Marie," says Mason.

"The most *obvious* answer."

"Rescuing," says Bingwen Bi, "has already been attempted and failed several times. Personally I think the best candidate to succeed may be the mysterious Englishman known as the Pimpernel –"

"What?" from Maggie. "Who?"

"If the Pimpernel has not acted yet, then the venture is a forlorn hope."

"I said *Who?*"

"The Pimpernel always leaves at the scene of his triumphs a scrap of paper with an imprint of the Scarlet Pimpernel flower. So I hear. And I hear that the Pimpernel can be very tall, but mostly isn't, which is puzzling."

"Ahem Rajit," says Mason, "but isn't the Pimpernel a literary invention? – *Oh I get it,* he's based on reality…"

Sharma, however, is speechless. Maggie Mo purses her lips.

But then Maggie shakes her head. "Not a word more. First I must think without any well-meant red herrings to lead me astray. Me and my HandyHan."

The most beautiful work of art in any world is Kitagawa Utamaro's *A Beauty Fondling Her Neck*, of 1790, created three years prior to Toshi Tanaka's arrival in Paris. Only half a world away, the masterpiece exists right now! Of the genre of beautiful-person-pictures called **Bijinga**. Real women of the time shaved off their eyebrows but, by jings as the Scots exclaim, Bijinga artists painted eyebrows nonetheless.

In the artwork the eyes of the apprentice Geisha – the *Maiko* girl – are slight slits just as should be so. Her nose

"The guards may watch the Queen use the potty any time they please. They foul the damp air by smoking."

is a single line. Her lips, two tiny rose petals. She beholds herself in a mirror while we gaze intoxicatedly at her neck revealed nakedly by her collar sliding down a smooth shoulder. Her babyish hand fondles its way up on to her nape. (We wish to push those fingers aside to behold the full curve; those delicate girly fingers tantalise us.) Some say that she's putting on powder; to our intent eyes there's no sign of powder. Her hair is black and lustrous, yet she wears no waxed wig – we see hundreds of individual hairs ascending tightly save where her white skin is trimmed by the neatest of barbering.

We reject any notion that Toshi's nape-of-the-neck fetish stems from him being carried upon his mother's back in traditional Nipponese fashion, thereby focusing most of his infantile attention upon a curvy bit of body (minus nipple). For a boy born in Common Era 2010, frankly the riding-the-back style is a bit outdated, especially for a boy with the heroic name Toshi. Testeroshi, almost, eh? If carrying baby boys *onbu*-style causes nape fixation, prior to the Meiji Era half the Japanese nation must have been yearning to lip their mothers' necks.

Nor could radiations released from the Fukushima tsunami nuclear meltdowns have twisted infant Toshi's libidinal fixation abnormally at the tender age of one. We seek a reasonable motivation. No fatuous linkages, such as of Jacques Lacan with lactation!

Unfortunately, we know nothing about Toshi's parents. Once Toshi has enough money, he eliminates their memory, we must suppose. Both mother and father in a sense castrated him, the father bestowing a penis that could be chopped off, gush of blood, the mother with her vagina wherein a penis is swallowed and drained until empty.

"Bondage photos, yes," Toshi tells the girl called Keiko who has a lucky character – 恵 – and who is eager for easy ¥en. Her red tartan high school miniskirt exposes bony knees. Her bunchy white socks flop upon pink sneakers. Her black hair is pixie-cut short.

"In an issue themed on sex-executions, sexcutions. In my basement studio I build a *gi-ro-chi-n*. I hang a heavy diagonal blade sharp as a katana made by Kaneshige."

"Ka-ka-ka…?"

"Idiot girl. 25K ¥en for a fotoshoot with my *gi-ro-chi-n*, hands and feet tied, juicy peach in mouth to bite on. Then plucked chicken chopped by my blade, desu né? Pics of your neck in nock or nook of the French device, tied hands outstretching, so da né?"

Keiko's head bobs acquiescence like a beckoning ceramic cat's mechanised paw. Toshi places between her cherry lips a lit joint of mariweed, which she sucks awkwardly.

Down in his basement Toshi modified the standard guillotine design in one respect by making the wooden neck-clamp or lunette quickly detachable, replaceable by an identical shape in tough transparent plastic should one so wish. Below is a big brown basket for harvesting tea, wovenly robustly.

Keiko easily found the office-cum-dwelling of Tanaka Toshi-san in Takada District, Toshima ward, Tokyo. Toshima and Toshi: sheer coincidence, elective affinity, cheap rent in a roughish neighbourhood?

Ah but we can all guess how this is *bound* to turn out, eh? Intersection of nape and notch for neck. Toshi's compulsion gripping him ever more magnetically. Fatal temptation. The electrical jerk of Cathexis! Slicing so divine. Blood blooming. Lucky Keiko's head jumping. Sublime! Propelled by arterial spouts, bouncing into the basket.

After a couple of weeks, a neighbour complains about pong. Soon the TMPD, the Tokyo Police, are on Toshi's tail. But he's already way ahead, the bulk of his wealth secure in prepaid elektrowallet, password ANTOINETTE1793, for him unforgettable. First destination, Oxford UK. For years the naughty young French Queen, that Viennese strawberry cream tart, has been in his inner sights and the Chinese Time Machine in his newsfeeds ever since *The People's Daily* published its authorised scoop about Professor Lin Quinan's breakthrough at Beijing's Time Institute. Let's be thankful that a responsible nation with a deep understanding of history has the key to time rather than a bunch of Johnny-Come-Lately cowboys, or a gang of Rasputins.

In the hope of spotting Toshi Tanaka, our trio become very familiar with the whole route which the tumbril cart takes to the 'national razor'. That circuitous journey starts in the courtyard outside the disgustingly mouldy and clamourous Concièrgerie prison on City Island. For maximum public visibility, the cart proceeds along rue de Palais to the Money Changers Bridge. After crossing the river the tumbril crawls along a quay past stenchy tanners' shops, and then... **that's enough topography of the Terror** it's a full hour until we rumble into Revolution Square, coinciding with the boom of the noon cannon at the Palais Royale.

Although the vilest insults may be hurled, nobody tosses any eggs or tomatoes. To ensure order, thirty thousand armed soldiers line the route. Consequently polished aristocrats, hands tied behind their backs, ignore the sea of inferiors and quip bon mots while inadvertently jostling one another due to passage over cobbles.

Not all tumbril passengers are aristos by any means. They might as easily be bakers' wives guilty of having flour on their fingers – *obviously* for powdering the Queen's hair rather than for putting a baguette in the belly of the mob. Or they can be peasants who were hoeing liberated land when the police of a distant inquisition arrived to arrest the rustics for something incomprehensible.

From our trio's base on Royal Road (renamed Revolution) they attend several days' of guillotinings to become *au fait* with the circumstances of the unfortunate.

Tricoleur flags blossom from all possible windows. Monsieur Sanson, the hereditary state executioner sporting his favourite posh blue fashiongear, has a couple of 'valets' to assist him up on stage.

That stage, bigger than a boxing ring, is like a stout multi-legged table. Two sides are curtain-walled with blank wood. The other two sides are open, allowing easy though stooping access to storage beneath. The long laundry basket into which headless bodies are tumbled slides down a ramp, with a springy hatch, to the underworld, reminiscent mutatis mutandis of what was underneath the Colosseum in Rome as regards disposal of newly dead corpses.

Sanson was training his firstborn Gabriel in the family trade but last year the youth slipped in blood and tumbled offstage, breaking his neck, quite a downer for Dad along with Dad developing kidney pangs and pee problems, so Bingwen Bi hears. Bi would recommend the executioner to dose with *huang qi* – that's astragalus to you – except for Bi's reluctance to branch out professionally in case this lowers the tone of his establishment or makes doctors jealous. Second son Henri Sanson is now the executioner's apprentice and heir. Despite Gabriel's demise the boxing ring hasn't been fitted with any posts and safety ropes.

The Queen's execution will be a special gala occasion, with her the mocked star in a cart of her own. Ordinarily during the Terror tumbrils plural run like future omnibuses between the prison and the guillotine.

Our trio's first outing coincides with a busy day of death, kicking off with a dozen males and females from all estates in life forming a queue. Already the tumbril, pulled by a white horse and preceded by a vainglorious officer, is leaving to bring another batch.

From beyond the rows of musket-toting soldiers arises an outcry of...

"Vive la République – !"
"Ça ira – !"
...as well as scurrilities:
"Salope – !
"Salaud – "
"Pouffy Ass – !
From close at hand:
"Garn, let her go! She's only a kid!"
Din ebbs. Moods are so volatile.

Mechanically Sanson receives the presumed servant girl, bundles her up the stairs which killed his own son. Her name is read, her offence. He tips her prone upon the positioning plank, secures the lunette. Other side, Henri pulls on her hair to be sure she stays in place, provoking a yelp. He might likewise have tugged her ears. Papa tugs twin ropes. Blade falls. Blood gushes. Into the basket goes her head. Already Henri's picking her head up by the hair to display briefly from one corner then from the next of the stage as his father descends to meet his next customer, while a valet resets the apparatus. Can Sanson keep this up all day?

The din rises as regards the girl.
"Boooooooo – !"

Noise ebbs out of curiosity as a thin old man is borne up the steps by his armpits. Our trio disperse as their best chance of spotting Tanaka. Like police spies on the look-out. Indeed just so. But a future police.

Excitedly, Sharma hastens into their apartment. Under his arm is tucked the *Moniteur Universel*, daily organ of the

"25K ¥en for a fotoshoot with my gi-ro-chi-n, hands and feet tied, juicy peach in mouth to bite on."

Committee of Public Safety – *The Execution News*, so to speak – even as he carries brioche and a brie for their breakfast. Down goes the shopping upon a drum table.

"Maggie," he pants, "I saw a *very* tall gent... posh to judge by his high top hat on which I glimpsed a token tricoleur ribbon! I thought *just maybe* –"

Immediately alert, "So you followed this tall man?"

"Yes, yes, Colonel Mo." Official duties, now. "To Law Street, former Richelieu. I wrote down the number. Mile and a bit from here."

"And you did the shopping beforehand or after?"

The Queen's execution will be a special gala occasion, with her the mocked star in a cart of her own.

"Bread and brie took but a mo. Um, Colonel. If we're to mount surveillance shouldn't we eat first?"

"Well riposted, Rajit. We shall take turns. So cut yourself a cheese sandwich and trot off back to that place. Mason and myself to follow in a couple of hours. We'll find you. If he's secretly the Pimpernel, the tall toff may be a vital contact for Tanaka in the matter of snatching away the Queen at the very last moment. Well done!"

Fortunately for Sharma a smart café, adorned with fluted Corinthian columns between which big mirrors multiply the clientele, sits diagonally opposite the target address. Marble tables, dressy citizen waiters. Life can be good when giving you lemons. Sharma sits for a long while, sipping, consulting a notebook, glancing out of the window across the street every thirty seconds as if he's a silent metronome. Customers come in to enjoy a lemonade or a liqueur or a cup of coffee plus chocolate; customers go. Sharma orders a coffee and a couple of chocs to pay more for his continuing presence. He cannot alas eat his sandwich.

Little does Sharma know, but the proprietress in her ample apple-green gown – Mme Honorine Grosgrain, rosy cheeks pocked from pox but in a peculiarly attractively way, delightfully dimply like a fruit for sweet devouring, and a tricoleur ribbon in her hair; you shan't cut off *this* pretty head, tu m'entend? – she's one of many well-wishers of the Queen.

Many well-wishers there are indeed! Common women of the Halles market send flowers and fruit lovingly to the Queen's cell. Hundreds of hairdressers do their hapless best to help the Queen escape; due to her years of huge hairstyles Marie-Antoinette-Josèphe-Jeanne of Austria-Lorraine may well be their patron saint, rather than Mary Magdalene. Barber blokes too. A Swedish count never loses hope of leading a troop of cavalry to spring Marie Antoinette free; meanwhile he hobnobs with cabbies just in case. Police agents uncover so many conspiracies.

Accordingly Mme Honorine Grosgrain, from her comfy gilded throne of a Shepherdess chair, is keeping her eye upon the Hindu. Across the road, as she knows, a luxurious flat is owned by an English milord. A 'roast-beef' immune, so it seems, to investigations by the Paris police. A rich man who appears to be entirely a creature of fashion whenever he walks upon the street. He's oblivious, so it seems, to the Revolution, apart from a token tricoleur ribbon. He's tall and strapping; people avoid bumping the Brit. How the milord might occupy his days, apart from dressing perfectly, does not occur to Honorine Grosgrain who spends her own days similarly, lounging impressively, surveying her lemonade domain.

At that moment an oriental woman enters and quickly seats herself beside the Hindu to whisper to the dusky fellow. How very interesting.

But wait: across Law Street-lately-Richelieu saunters Milord his very self heading in the direction of *Café Honorine* for the first time ever. The Roast-beef strolls casually while other street users part like the Red Sea. That walking cane which Milord idly toys with on his way, its handle a long-eared hare's head in silver, may include a Toledo blade.

Wait even further: for as the Hindu lays a hand on the oriental woman in case she hasn't noticed – she suppresses a lethal stiffening of her fingers – down along Richelieu-now-Law blinks a momentary glimpse of Toshi Tanaka. The porn-ninja must be intent upon visiting the Pimpernel at home! Having made contact with the tall Toff alias the secretive heroic Pimpernel due to prior historical knowledge. Maggie is right!

If only phones exist in this era, to avert French farce!

Molly Mo and her two Oxford dons have struggled with the historicity of the Pimpernel, for the HandyHan troublesomely supports this or denies this on alternate days.

Here's just one sample altercation, or let's say discussion, such as might take place in a Parisian salon presided over by a refined but feisty Enlightenment lady, freely open to all social classes if sufficiently educated. Colonel Mo is in fine command of her own Club of Three in their flat in Royal Revolution Road.

"So tell me, Dr Sharma, is Sir Percy the Pimpernel, supposedly two persons in one – is he fictional or factual? My HandyHan alternates the two versions."

"Isn't there something called *superposition*?" hazards Rajit. "Until you open the cat's cardboard box? And the cyanide gas either kills or it doesn't?"

"Don't you mean if the cyanide gas is *released* or it isn't?" from Prof Mason. "Surely cyanide gas *always* kills a cat? Followed, if so," he adds cleverly, "by killing the observer too as he opens the box to inspect! I happen to know from – no it wasn't Agatha Christie herself – that cyanide gas rises, as it's lighter than air. Which puts us right back where we were to start with, eh?"

"This does not help!" snaps Maggie. "Or... does it?"

And now convergence is upon us, for Sir Percy slash Pimpernel is manifesting himself in reality – as a feast of a man wearing garments worth dozens of guineas. Into the coffee house he comes, pauses only momentarily to glance around, calls to a waiter in quite passable French, "Cup of your best Martinique, pray," then insinuates himself towards Sharma's and Maggie's table, where he doffs his top hat to the lady.

In drawly English, "Madam, I take it upon myself to introduce you to Sir Percy Blakeney of Richmond in the County of Surrey. Your Indian friend appears to much admire my modest pied-à-terre in

Paris as if wishing to purchase it. May I seat myself here, to hear your offer, Sir?" The fop whinnies at his own wit like a young horse.

Sharma, however, is unabashed. "Can't a chap pass a couple of hours in peace in a caff, watching the world go by?" Not a Hindu voice at all. A British voice.

A waiter duly positions a gilded chair for Sir Percy's derrière, and Milord settles.

"Nay Sir, you weren't watching the world, but rather my door and windows. Odd's fish! Explain yourself, Sir!"

A porcelain cup of coffee arrives.

"You may put that on my bill," Sharma says in a superior way. Plenty of assignats to burn, eh?

The waiter inclines his head monolingually.

Maggie's throat ripples like some marionettiste's and her lingo-collar utters, "Mettez-la sur notre facture, Monsieur."

For the first time, Sir Percy pays attention to Maggie Mo.

"Pardon me but I took you for a harlot," he brays.

Provocation enough for Sharma to show his colours, so to speak – to reveal who and what is keeping watch on a possible Pimpernel's flat. At all costs let Sir P's privacy be protected! If necessary by rapiers at dawn in Students' Meadow, le Pré-aux-Clercs. With his yard of slim Toledo steel and his long reach, Sir Percy can scarcely lose.

Yet that victory may betray the supposedly effete Toff as being a dashing daring genius of swordsmanship, not to mention of subterfuge... So maybe Sir Percy must allow himself to suffer, with a squeal, a little flesh wound? Little does Sir P imagine how Rajit Sharma never held a sword in his life – wore yes, during the St Helena escapade, but never flourished steel.

Scenting imminent bloodshed, Mme Grosgrain hefts a rolling pin – the wooden dowel sort – camouflaged in black Chantilly lace, rises from her throne, and... simultaneously or thereabouts Toshi Tanaka presses his palms to the windowpanes. The mighty presence of Sir Percy captures the Nipponese pornpic publisher's attention to the exclusion of all else and inside he rushes precipitately.

"Ohayoo gozaimasu, Sir Percy-san!"

Chantilly lace may easily provoke a police spy. That's due to its posh aristo pedigree. After Marie Antoinette and the last gasp of her patronage get the chop, all of the lace-makers in nearby Chantilly are likewise chopped, such a shame, all those skilled threadsmiths snipped short; we hiss at that.

A puritanical Jacobin police spy named Pellerin – *Gaspard* Pellerin, if you insist – is sipping cold coffee when the proprietress raises that lacy black standard of a club. She's only intent on peace and order. Even so! Gaspard Pellerin is ambitious for more attention from the authorities, especially from Citizen Chauvelin. From Gaspard's waistband comes a flintlock pistol, the short sort.

"Citizeness!" he shouts out. "Lay down your weapon in the name of the Republic and of the People! I reveal that I am a Policeman!"

To see the fellow draw a pistol, which might or might not fire at the Pimpernel-in-secret, impels Tanaka to pull out his wakizashi and toss it at Pellerin's gun-hand. To use his blade as a *bo shuriken* is a clever ninja ploy but we aren't going into all of that stuff right now. We merely mention that the so-called 'sword-saint' Musashi Miyamoto famously killed a duelling opponent by tossing his short sword. Toshi did pay attention to this famous feat.

The tossed wakizashi neatly amputates Pellerin's hand at the wrist. Amidst failed fingers the pistol falls – bounces – discharges its ball of lead. There follows a truly French ricochet from off a chandelier. Crying out, a waiter claps a hand to his blooded shoulder, his silver tray dropping clangingly. Maggie is already peeling from her elegant chair to hit the floor and roll, and to come up outstretching to clutch that wakizashi by its handle of goosebumpy stingray skin (alias *shagreen* although this shagreen's dyed reddish). Only the best shagreen for Toshi Tanaka.

Oh his chagrin to see his own blade in a Chinese hand! To halt his rush he must dig in his heels and somersault backwards, another ninja skill. This brings his brow into collision with Mme Grosgrain's rolling pin, oops, so he reels a bit.

Some ladies customers squeal, some men bray like donkeys. Porcelain cascades. One chap overturns his table to be a shield. Another shows steely sangfroid; he may be au fait with just how damn long it takes to reload and recharge such a pistol with ball and powder. A couple of teenage waiters, twins by the look of them, make themselves scarce in a rush out the front way.

As for Gaspard Pellerin, he faints due to surprise at the bright blood pulsing from his stump. Wonderful is the speed with which Mme Grosgrain assesses, discards her lace-wrapped club, and surges to her kitchen. She returns bravely with a brazier of hot coals on to which she forces the bloody stump to staunch. It sizzles. It smokes. Gaspard recovers consciousness shrieking but – mark our words, later on, equipped with a prosthetic hand the same Citizen Gaspard Pellerin will become famous as Claw of the Law, chief of police regardless whichever regime's in power, royalty included, a true survivor. He will wed widow Grosgrain, without a doubt.

"Go away!" Tanaka shrieks at Maggie. "Mind your own business! I swear I'll alter no event!" The Tokyo photoporn king reels even more so, back out into the street. Quickly he rights his personal compass and launches himself off down an alley, as a curious crowd begins to gather outside the café due to the gunshot and turmoil within.

Life can be good when giving you lemons.

What a kerfuffle! Such confusion! Cat among the pigeons, pachyderm in the porcelain shop. And in all of this mêlée, where is Sir Percy right now?

"Where's Percy Blakeney gone to?" hisses Sharma to Mason who tried to overturn their table for a shield while Rajit wrestled to keep it and the crockery upright.

Colonel Mo is back beside them, custodian of the wakizashi now, never to let it go even if blood will stain her faded quilted coat. "*Where's* the Pimp? *Where's the Pimp?* You know who I mean!"

Sharma concentrates, going cross-eyed. "Dunno. But two waiters left. Young brothers. Lads in waiter uniforms. Didn't notice them earlier…"

Oh his chagrin to see his own blade in a Chinese hand!

"Good. Let me think, let me think…" She closes her eyes. "Is that how the Pimp carries it off? Is it? Can the man and his clothes come together, like the plumage and the pheasant?"

"Clothes maketh the man," quotes Sharma, "especially in the case of a dandy, a Beau Brummel avant le jour."

"Can the clothing and the person literally metamorphose – ?"

Maggie strikes her brow, making yet another great leap of deduction which is like the goddess of wisdom Athena emerging fully armed from the forehead of Zeus.

"Of course of course! Toshi Tanaka doesn't want to rescue Marie Antoinette at all. He wants to be in there up close as can be, participating. The only way he can wrangle that is by using the Scarlet Pimpernel's smoke and mirrors talents along with his own ninja skill to position him right there upon the execution stage at the perfect moment – yes, as assistant guillotinist might be his perfect role – which requires deluding Sir Percy to believe that the Queen can be saved at the eleventh hour and fifty-ninth minute and spirited away!"

Prof Mason of Oxford Univ can only boggle at the depth of these deductions. Recovering some of his wits, "If that's so, surely we can return home right away, um, Colonel? No need to stay to make sure the Queen gets her hair well and truly parted."

"I think not, my good Prof. What, we irresponsibly leave Toshi Tanaka in the past, him blessed with our own future know-how of the rise of Napoleon? Mais non mon Empereur, do not invade Russia, very bad notion. I'll explain exactly why, mon Emp… but by the way, first may I have another immunity for guillotining a pretty peasant girl? Please ask – HandyHan, who will Napoleon's Police Chief be?"

<*Foosh foosh foosh*> – a noise like an airplane winding a tough rubber band up prior to take-off, doubtless a hydraulic sound…is HandyHan having some speech problem? – ah but now here comes clearly: <*Pellerin, Gaspard Pellerin.*> "Tell Police Chief Pellerin please. Tell Pellerin to sign a pardon!" Maggie mocks.

"I am Pellerin," a voice cries out in anguish. The fellow with the roast wrist now writhing on the floor. That fellow! The very same!

"Calmez-vous," Widow Grosgrain coos, down upon her knees beside Pellerin. Tenderly, "Calmes-toi." She disappears the pistol underneath her gown.

In the street, musket-toting soldiers are paying ever closer heed to the coffee cake choc café.

"Let's scarper," urges Mason. "If that's okay with you, Colonel, Sir and Madam?" Mason is a bit old-school.

Hiding the wakizashi within her coat, Maggie kneels by pained Pellerin and shouts at his ear, "**Citizen Gaspard, tell your police superior to find *Tanaka Toshi* oriental man *he is Nipponese NOT Chinese* hiding somewhere in Paris. Monsieur Tanaka-san has a plan to free the Queen. Let's go, guys.**"

Every decent café kitchen needs a back door for escapes. Plus to put out rubbish for rats.

Bingwen Bi inclines his head at Maggie in a brief bow. "I'm humbly obliged to you for exonerating all and any Chinese people in Paris from the crime of queen-freeing."

"I was *emphatic* on that point, rest assured."

The Factor of Chinoiserie – *cum* secret ambassador of the Heavenly Throne in the person of the long-ruling far-away Qianlong Emperor – is receiving Maggie Mo and her duo of Oxford dons in the reception room of *Choses Chinoises*. Having brought a lacquered tray bearing green tea and delicious signature date buns some while ago, Precious Hairpin has this time settled to hear secrets. Foresightfully Bingwen Bi is grooming his daughter for succession should her sire get the chop.

If only Maggie could show Bingwen Bi on her HandyHan the sheer reach by 2055 of the 'Belt-and-Road' railway and shipping trade routes! One Belt One Road! Yi Dai Yi Lu! The belt isn't a belt and the road isn't a road but who cares, it's epic. Who cares if the name fluctuates.

"Far from me to risk your reputation," Maggie assures. "We must neutralise the Nipponese nape-pervert." Unaccountably she giggles. Surely hashish is in the date cakes today!

Bingwen Bi must co-operate with the bearer of a Chuán Guó Xǐ Heirloom Seal of the Realm, yet he may certainly query details for clarification.

"Respectfully, Almost-Highest-Lady, did you imply that the big gwaïlo Roast-Beef became two very-similar smaller waiters? Before your very own eyes?"

"Very similar or verisimilar," comments Mason.

"Don't split hares," from Sharma, imitating long ears.

Hashish relaxes a person, making them fatuous, yet also opening mental doors. Is mild drugging of an Heirloom Seal Bearer within the permitted repertoire of a loyal and ingenious Factor?

Precious Hairpin, Baozhai, amazes the visitors by asking Maggie in very decent singsong English, rising and falling, "Do your two buffoon jesters help you think clearly, please? The way that Dongfang Shuo helped Emperor Wu of Han?"

Precious Hairpin's papa looks modestly pleased; Maggie, disconcerted.

"What *exactly* did you witness?" she asks Sharma, who is busily pinching himself.

"I saw two lads in waiter togs. Like twins. They left very fast, out the front way."

"Sir Percy was no longer to be seen?"

Once again Sharma crosses his eyes. "I – don't – know."

From Bingwen Bi, "Both of you believe that the Gwailo Milord *including his clothing* metamorphosed into two smaller persons dressed differently from himself – and that this kind of capability is at the root of the Pimpernel's amazing successes."

Maggie confesses, "A voice haunts me. It's trying to say something like, 'When you eliminate the impossible, whatever remains, no matter how improbable, must be the truth.' Whoever will say that? In this case, the improbable appears *to be* the impossible!"

Mason nods. "Here's a new one for your *Book of Changes*, eh?"

"You drug us un peu." More of a comment from Maggie than an accusation.

"To open one's understanding," allows Bingwen Bi.

"I permit this," says Maggie. "We need some derangement of the senses to apprehend the nature of the Pimpernel."

"And to apprehend the gwailo himself?"

"I have no mission regarding the gwailo himself. I merely require the Queen to die by the guillotine, and for Toshi Tanaka to –"

" – to fail? Whereby the Queen might somehow contrastingly *live*? You say 'the gwailo himself' – might that be him*selves*?"

Maggie pinches the ball of her thumb in a disciplined way. "Can the executioner Sanson be *bribed*? Bribed to *ensure* that the Queen will die? Better still, bribed to kill the Japanese pervert in the flagrant act due to disgust?" Another self-pinch. "To what extent does Sir Percy choose his disguise – or does the disguise choose itself? This is worthwhile resin, Bingwen Bi."

"Let us acknowledge Precious Hairpin in that regard, for the Big Ma," sketching in the air with a quick forefinger the characters 大麻 or Tao-ma, making a sort of Han pun alluding to Maggie, cannabis, and other considerations.

"Uptime we use acupuncture needles more scientifically for interrogation, rather than a narcotic…"

Mason is gazing transfixed at a glazed porcelain camel, blue and orange, from the Tang time. Sharma examines his own fingers as though he can read the faint swirl of prints.

Says the Factor, "Hereditary High Executioner Sanson has great expenses and little income, so I hear. I hear he is fed up with his job-for-life, and aches to retire. Sanson was grooming his firstborn son Gabriel to succeed him. Back in July, Gabriel alas slipped in blood while showing a newly severed head to the crowd and thus fell off the scaffold, breaking his neck."

They have already seen Sanson in all his glory up on the scaffold on the job. A tall muscular figure almost worth of Sir Percy Blakeney himself, quite the dandy too, muscles pumped by decades of wielding the mighty sword that preceded the guillotine; a sword tiresomely to be sharpened anew after every single execution to keep its edge. Swanky blue frock coat these days with wide white cravat, silk stockings, and bright buckled shoes, tricorne hat, sword at his side for self-defence. And this on his lack of salary!

Mason giggles zanily. "Biter bitten."

"Sanson's second son Henri is now learning the necessary skills displayed by his papa."

"Isn't papa paid enough for cutting off heads?" Sharma asks, looking up. "Eeenie meenie miney money. Haha!"

"I hear his pay is gained mainly by selling possessions of the newly dead. At his own expense he must provide and maintain the guillotine. I hear he must pay half a dozen assistants to perform repairs and I know not what else. I hear he sells newly guillotined bodies for research, and shorn hair to wigmakers. I hear he himself is a person of culture, cursed inescapably to be the official state killer. He appears to be a person of honour. I never heard of him accepting bribes. For what purpose? To accept a handsomely paid substitute victim at the eleventh hour?"

"It's all a bit publicly visible," remarks Mason, "up there on the scaffold. I have a headache."

Maggie says in a dreamy way, "We should stay inconspicuous for a while. We may have attracted too much attention at the café. Admirable Bingwen Bi, may we leave in your keeping the whacky zashy? After a year you can display the blade in your shop window if you wish."

"That might be profitable," allows the Factor, "except that thirty years ago I believe Madame de Pompadour was a great enthusiast for what wraps the handle of that sword. Due to Madame de Pomp's enthusiasm, Louis XV's court was full of luxury objects covered in the same costly skin. Common folk might see such a *Galuchat* handle in my window and hiss with disapprobation at royal extravagance."

<*Galuchat?*> Maggie subvoces at her hopefully hidden HandyHan.

<**Sharkskin, Mistress. Named after an expert tanner of Paris whom the Pompadour patronised.**>

"How damn bizarre," murmurs Mason in the direction of Maggie's knees. "Don't Froggy sword hilts use sharkskin, HandyHan?"

"Yes, Servant of She."

"So where's the fuss? I think Bee Bee is prevaricating. Maybe on principle! You hold the whatnot, Madame Mo. The seal thing. For commanding."

Bingwen Bi inclines himself. "Things I do hear, as I may have mentioned several times. I am aware that you do not tell me all that you might. Otherwise I might possibly act at variance with my duty, and with your own mission, so as to protect Precious Hairpin from possible harm."

Is this a request, or a hidden threat? Which? Which!

Precious Hairpin herself pipes up: "My father has thought much about the nature of time and about history, most of which is a tale of pain and death. Here, I am a peculiar demoness living in exile within a barbaric hell."

"But you're a beauty," declares Sharma, somewhat druggedly. "And clever."

"Before you came today to eat special date cakes, my father knew nothing about how Sir Percy Person might divide himself into two, or three, or more. Along with his garments. Now my father does know. What difference does this knowledge make to our own diplomatic mission and mandate? We did not expect this. What else may we not expect?"

More of a request this time, than a demand.

Sharma blusters, "The situation here in France will settle down. Stay here to survive. Not for much longer. Robespierre's days are numbered. And all of his ilk. Soon there'll be a French Emperor –"

"*What – ?*" from father and daughter alike.

"Rajit, take care!" exclaims Maggie Mo.

"There'll come war all over Europe for a while. My advice is stay here in Paris, ma belle, et père. Continue to import. War won't become total during your lives. Shall we?" asks Rajit, nodding towards Maggie's knee where the Handy-Han hides.

Temptation is great. Maggie has it in her power to show to this faithful Factor the glorious global future of China – vaulting over the two-hundred year slump of shame and humiliation due to set in. She can uplift the secret ambassador as well as his clever daughter.

"Train, planes, and automobiles?" hints Rajit. Seal-bearer Maggie certainly can convey heavenly thanks to the Factor, even if she cannot take father and daughter 'home' for a true thanksgiving.

Or can she?

"But will they *see* a *train* and know what it is?" from Mason. "Will they see a plane see a plane see a plane – "

"You're rhyme-trapped, Professor," Maggie cuts through his comment. She can still be sharp. "Admirable Bingwen Bi and praiseworthy Precious Hairpin, I will show you some wonders in colour and motion of future China, to reward your loyalty. In exchange you will both observe carefully on the day the ex-Queen now called Widow Capet loses her head, from as close up as possible – and intervene if need be, and if possible, to catch Tanaka."

Without further ado, Maggie whips into view her "HandyHan!" at a suitable angle for dad and daughter to see. "Show Chinese supertrains crossing landscapes and cities. Let there be Hanzi characters visible – from before simplification, the old characters – no no cancel that's silly. Go! –

" – and next show Chinese planes taking off, flying over Chinese cities, landing at giant airports..."

Wow! Wa! Whoop! with amazed yet dignified composure.

Presently the Factor says: "Second-to-highest-Lady, did you and your gwailos arrive here inside a box-kite with hard wings such as we saw just now?" Collars compete: <...within *mu yuan*> <inside the windharp>. "Where could you bring it down to earth? Where could you hide it?"

"Not a plane, no. We came in a sort of *hun yi* sphere." Maggie gestures interacting rung-hoops such as compose an armillary sphere evoking the central kingdom's five-star polymath genius Zhang Heng – except for its interior rotating rings being *nested superposed* thus allowing for passenger space within [REDACT THIS BY ORDER # 2055 OF BEIJING TIME INSTITUTE].

"Of course," says Bingwen Bi, "any adequately educated Chinese person knows much about Zhang Heng."

"Harrumph," from Mason.

Precious Hairpin says brightly, "I shall take my binocular lorgnette to the Queen's execution for clarity in case soldiers press me away."

Sharma is becoming smitten. Back in academic Oxford he never met anyone like Hairpin, nor previously in Brumingham. Rajit Sharma is skinny and brown, a head taller than Prof Mason. Daughter Baozhai is just slightly plump, endowed genetically with what one calls almond eyes, skin of best blancmange rose-blushy upon the cheeks, couple of delightful dimples. She seems to favour Sharma with glances that are at once modest yet provocative, although he may be a bit -stoned. Hash helps to enchant. You think the effect has gone away just when another wavelet washes up on your shore.

Bingwen Bi casually mentions in Sharma's general direction, "Full fifty years ago our cultured Qianlong Emperor, Hongli who still reigns, especially appreciated among all his other consorts the frugal kindly Lady Fuca who wore artfully crafted flowers in her hair in preference to jewels. She fondled silkworms."

"A precious consort," comments Precious Hairpin, "is an economical consort."

"And subsequently Hongli adored beautiful Fragrant Concubine Rong Fei, a Moslem captured by Chinese soldiers after they killed her Uyghur husband. Rong was a huntress, although not hunting for any replacement husband. She was a skilled horsewoman."

"Uyghur," repeats Rajit, seeking significance.

"For the most part Hongli has been a vastly benevolent and beneficial ruler of China, along with a few unavoidable minor genocides around the edges, prunings really, recoverable from within a century, all for the sake of unity, reconciliation, and harmony. Anyway, Hongli insisted that his beloved kidnapped courtesan widow must become happy, even building her a Moslem mosque in her lovely garden. Presumably with a eunuch *I-am* dwelling within. Apparently the fragrance of her skin was astonishing. On her long journey in a closed comfy cart to the capital she washed daily in camels' milk. Or was washed."

"I should not hope to bathe in camel's milk," Baozhai confides at Sharma.

"Nor shall you be forced to!" Rajit declares gallantly.

Bingwen Bi gazes levelly at Colonel Mo. "If Precious Hairpin and myself successfully help yourselves capture or kill the Nipponese pervert you must swear upon the Heirloom Seal of the Realm to take my daughter forward in time with you inside the *hun yi* sphere. Which is hidden where, incidentally?"

Hashmark hashmark where's the harm? Bingwen Bi won't go carelessly to gape at the time pod. He won't invite being followed by Tanaka in camo cloaking – oh we'd better mention that ninja semi-visibility aspect to Bingwen! What if Bingwen arranges for an ambush inside the Luxembourg Gardens at the overgrown orchard...? Hmm. Hmm.

"Do you promise upon the Heirloom Seal?" pressses Bingwen. "Do you?"

"Um, Precious Baozhai, is this what *you* want? To go to the future in time where you will know nobody?"

"Whom do I know closely here in Paris? In the future I believe I will know Scholar Sharma?"

"You certainly shall!"

"Calm yourself, Rajit. But, Precious, you will never see your father again. Only perhaps his grave, perhaps with an inscription, a poem to you."

"I go where my parent points."

"The Heirloom Seal, Second-Greatest-Lady..."

"Yes yes." Which Maggie produces from a pocket of her Guoanbu uniform beneath the soiled quilty coat. "Loyalty ties *you* here, Ambassador Factor..."

"I'm not so sure about that!" Bingwen Bi surprises her by exclaiming. "Lately I hear how our military and cultural mastermind the Qianlong Emperor may be beguiled and befuddled in his dotage by corrupt officials. Especially I finger the super-rich extortioner Heshen! I hear things and I read things. By the blessing of Heaven I benefit from close friendships with knowledgeable persons in the ports of Nont and of Bordo."

"You certainly don't belong to the Plain Red Banner," deduces Maggie.

"Correct, Second-Greatest-Lady. I yearn for Heshen to be accused."

"I might guess that you gave up your banner affiliation in order to trade in goods as a cover for being a covert Chinese ambassador – a sacrifice for your country, although in line with your own aesthetic enthusiasms?"

Thanks to collars Sharma and Mason understand what is spoken though not what on earth any of it means.

Bingwen Bi inclines his head. "All is complex regarding the *braiding* – the plaiting, the interlacing – of Manchu lineages and Han lineages, what with so many adoptions and inductions."

Likewise incomprehensible. Still, Rajit has a go, taking a punt at it as an Oxford man might, knowing enough not to stand on the slippery platform end to pole the punt. Such wisdom is mostly lost in the mists amidst bright yellow peddle-ducks for the Han package-tourists.

"So is a Han man more than a Manchu?"

Oops, splash. Embarrassing. Rajit's stoned. Precious Hairpin does simper but quickly interposes four fingers as a furled fan to hide her lips.

Maggie Mo is keen to delve into what Bingwen Bi yearns for, so she asks Handy-Han in Guangdongese, for privacy – which we can reveal – "Briefly tell me the end years of extortionist Heshen."

<*Qianlong Emperor abdicates in 1796 Common Era out of filial respect so as not to rule longer than his father ruled. He will continue directing everything from offstage. Only when he dies in 1799 will his successor Yongyan the Jiaqing Emperor be able to arrest Heshen and investigate his enormous wealth, twelves times that of China's entire treasury, and allow Heshen to choose between being slowly and dishonourably sliced to death in public, or suicide at home by hanging for which Heshen will use a golden silken rope on February 22 1799 C.E.*>

Hmm, that's about six years from now.

Inform Bingwen Bi of the outcome? Aye, and consequently inform those associates in Nont and Bordo, and *their* associates wherever, without precise details to be sure...

Stay silent? Do without help which might make all the difference?

Or perform an extraction, as spy masters and dentists both put it?

As if reading Maggie's thoughts, Bingwen Bi clears his throat. "Ahem. My trusted acquaintance in Nont is amply qualified to take over my position permanently here in Paris, as Factor and as secret ambassador. He can be here from Nont within a week. He's a Han with a clever hen and two cocky chicks."

"Oh Father! So we *can* see one another in future. After Rajit and I..." She trails off. Lambs' eyes.

"Worthy Factor, our *hun yi* sphere is hidden at the Luxembourg Gardens. It's camouflaged by 'Shimmer' though you can touch it with a blind hand. In future China you'll be pensioned very comfortably. So many scenic sights to visit by supertrain from Tibet to Taiwan. So many cities of twenty million prosperous citizens buying things and enjoying. So many zoos full of romping creatures. So many joyful ethnic dances. So many tasty festival buns. Billions of pretty flowers blooming. And a hotel in Heaven itself, being a new little moon in the sky the size of a pea seen at arm's length which you can travel to safely by big exploding bamboo baozhu rocket."

"And the Terracotta Army," adds Mason helpfully.

"What's that?" asks Bingwen Bi, mystified.

"Scholar Sharma," interrupts Precious Hairpin Baozhai, "will you squire me to a big baozhu rocket launch in future China? My father and I watch fireworks whenever we can."

How can Sharma resist such persuasions?

Wednesday October 16th 1793 C.E. is cloudy and cold. One might catch one's death wobbling on the plank seat of a cart, hands tied behind one's back, neck shorn of hair, paraded through Paris streets. Hair might impede the blade so that one's head doesn't come off completely. Sanson took scissors to Marie after tying her hands. He pocketed the lank locks, once the strawberry blond envy of France, to sell to wig-makers.

Raggy black robe, cap of mourning for her hubby who lost his head months and months earlier. Silly Louis tried to escape to Austria but en route he paid a shopkeeper with a banknote featuring the King's own face, so easy to compare.

Approaching what is currently Revolution Place we hear a rising wave of catcalls from drunken citizens paid by the Jacobins to jeer at Widow Capet.

"En avant!"

"Putain!"

She ignores all of that, keeping her long nose and stiff Habsburg lower lip snootily to the fore. That's true dignity. Shoulder to shoulder soldiers double-deep line her whole route and all around the scaffold platform not unlike a boxing ring. Anyone who as much as tosses a squashy tomato will be arrested within

> "We need some derangement of the senses to apprehend the nature of the Pimpernel."

seconds.

Staff officers walk ahead of the single white horse that pulls the tumbril. A trio of generals bring up the rear. It's a bit foggy.

Tumbril halts. Sanson in his best finery awaits her descent. Remarkably the exhausted ailing woman does accomplish this unaided. Due to wobbling she treads on his foot.

"Pardon me, Sir, that was not intended." Her last known words are polite and considerate. She's a gem.

Here and now in the crowd is a perfect moment when Sir Percy becomes less than a person – subhuman as well as into the butcher-smelly oval wicker basket where heads tumble. It's all so fast. Existence will cease in a trice or maybe after ten seconds down there, confused, concussed, a punched rabbit.

Onlookers see clearly how Sanson

One might catch one's death wobbling on the plank seat of a cart, hands tied behind one's back, neck shorn of hair, paraded through Paris streets.

transhuman. No longer merely here, no longer strictly now.

Sir Andrew Ffoulkes is there in the crowd along with his leader. Ffoulkes is disguised as a carter in rustic smock, distressed strong boots, wide flat cap. A spacious cloak will conceal the ex-Queen, calmed – if any need there be! – by inhaling sweet oil of vitriol from a soporific sponge, the more easily to bear her away. What Ffoulkes witnesses of Sir Percy's special moment he will never confide to the select circle of Sir Percy's other supporters, assuming he could put it into words. It causes a local cloud of confusion, of unknowing, of undecidability.

Like specially pavloved hounds, the Pimpernel instinctively tasks its self and its self. He'll know himself again afterwards, after words regain sense. The strange-one-with-skills whose gossamer cloak *pixies* the view, so to speak, will block the descent of the blade using an ingenious multi-function tool made in future Switzerland, as Tanaka has shown to Sir Percy.

A flurry comes from the fog like a djinn of a dust devil upon a dune, and this devil divides into two, or into half or into halves, hard to say.

Marie's shoe comes off. Seizing her in a strong though helpful grip, Sanson propels her up the stairs and on to stage. To the footrest of the tiltboard he waddles her. An assistant ropes her for quick release. Does she notice the long rectangular wicker basket placed close for her headless body to be rolled into?

Over she goes so suddenly, to rest her neck on the wooden demilune and stare himself steps aside, yielding his role as executioner to son Henry. There comes a strange flurry. Does a body fall from the slippery stage the way Sanson's first son fell?

A hand tugs Marie's hair roughly by her cap to pull her neck further forward upon the demilune. She squeals in surprise and affront. This cruel tug reveals to her an oriental face. What she sees is inexplicable. A demonic eastern imp has descended from a gargoyle to snatch her soul away! Substituting itself for the basket attendant! How scrawny is Marie's shorn nape, how withered by hardships and pains. Yet a hand thrusts up a compact customised periscope higher than the wooden immobiliser, the better to gaze down at that nape. Spittle froths the lips of that oriental demon.

That reflector, which is no blade-deflector, never came from any Switzerland! Is Marie's last sight to be the glaze-eyed lust of Tanaka as the blade descends? As he achieves release, of the cathectic as well as of the moist kind! As a usurper, Tanaka must be in a lot of danger here. Namely danger of arrest, not of being killed on the spot. Law and order rules the land in this reign of terror.

Close by, Liberty sits on her plinth clutching a lance. What moment is the last of a life? Can there be a penultimate moment of expectation of the end? Like a quickie trailer before the reel (and the real) runs out? Awareness is never of the actual moment itself but of a moment just gone by into memory. Any memory recalled to mind is unreliable.

Can one witness one's own death, in a mirror, retarded just a tic by the speed of light, as the blade first bites the nape while the spinal column remains intact? No, for the reflection must first reach the eye. And be coded for the optic nerve. Then decoded. We think. We rethink. We unthink.

What the devil is *this* now? An arm which ends in a tightly bandaged stump is waving in the faces of the black-hatted red-coated musketmen who confront the milling crowd.

"Let me through, Lads! I'm Gendarmerie Agent Gaspard Pellerin. Criminal Tan-a-ka is up there. It's him as is tugging the hair of Widow Capet! The genuine scaffold assistant is underneath, dead or knocked out."

A gap opens in the double red line for Pellerin, to rush to the stairs waving one-handed a warrant signed days earlier by Robespierre himself. Beyond the cordon of soldiers is a swirling sea of people sporting dirty cockades. Over that way are the knitting women on their raised benches, market wives bitter at the disregard of them since their march to Versailles then back to Paris again victorious with captive monarchs.

A tranche of audience close to the tumbril surge in hope that some souvenir might drop such as a ribbon. The vast majority of gazes (apart from of soldiers whose backs are turned) are angled up at the stage. Who notices Mme Honorine Grosgrain rise to her full if modest height close to the stairway, after crawling speedily on hands and knees never mind her dignity or soiling her apple-green gown. In her left hand is Gaspard's flintlock pistol. It's cocked to fire, once. Honorine has been practising in her kitchen. Soon Gaspard will receive his first claw of iron. Honorine follows closely after Gaspard, up the stairs, while the true Sanson observes.

Later on, HandyHan will reveal how the General Police Bureau, where Gaspard hangs out in the Louvre Palace, is almost adjacent to the Committee of Public Safety where Robespierre roosts. A strong personal recommendation for hook-fitting by Red Robby causes the estimable surgeon Dupuytren of the Hôtel-Dieu Hospital to attend to the amputated Gaspard personally. This is the very same exalted Dupuytren who, HandyHan adds, will soon be treating Napoleon's hemorrhoids; the very same surgeon who writes the ground-breaking treatise *Artificial Anus*. An artificial claw will serve Gaspard well enough as Napoleon's and Everyone Else's Chief of Police come the due days. Such are the links in the web of life, spreading like the mycelium of a fungus.

Marie Antoinette's life still rests in the balance as she stares into the butchery basket whilst the erotomaniacal Tanaka gazes at her withered nape in the mirror, his manhood stiff to bursting, approaching juicyance, jouissance, enhanced enjoyment.

We use the term 'erotomaniacal' purely due to the word 'erotic' being used in conjunction with 'mania' and 'maniac' – not out of reference to **de Clérambault's Syndrome**, which is the delusion that someone of higher status is in love with you.

Who can fail to admire a French Alienist mind-doctor with the wondrous name of Gaëtan Henri Alfred Edouard Léon Marie Gatian de Clérambault? (*Marie* again! – how the web of the world trembles.) What a fellow. Psychoshrink, dab hand as a painter, professional photographer with umpteen photos of hysterics. Decorated warrior (Croix de Guerre) and authority on Moroccan tribal costumes as well as on the voluptuous draping of fabric, notably silk with which madwomen masturbate behind counters in posh shops. Enemy of gimmicky Surrealism. Post-structurally the 'father' of **Lacan**.

Afflicted by botched cataract surgery, Gaëtan Gatian de Croquembouche finally suicides by bullet in the mouth in 1934 aged 62 in his lonely home shared only with wax dolls dolled up by him in draped silk and other fabric, him being married to those female dolls fetishistically. Not even a blind man can miss his brain through his open bouche. Bang. Fin. Faster than for Marie, we suppose. Gaëtan Gatian de Clérambault's Alienism is out of fashion, Freudian psychoanalysis is in. Surrealists revel.

How long can we let the ex-Queen continue to cliffhang? Surely the poor lady has suffered enough. Time slows; the noise of the crowd is distant.

It is **Lacan**, Jacques Lacan – Jacques-*Marie* Lacan, actually, dandified connoisseur of gazelle girls, Lacan – who will say: "Suicide is the only deed capable of individual success."

So we must ask: What of the hypothetical suicide of a person divided, such as Sir Percy? A person who exhibits *dissociative symptoms*?

Watch this space!

A foggy ripple rumples any clarity of view. Within the crowd Sharma ventures to give a gentle squeeze to Precious Hairpin's hand. Moments later she reacts – with neither less pressure than more – in so doing losing her exact fix on where Bingwen Bi had been a moment before.

She gasps. "Where's my father!"

There's a fuzz. There's a buzz. The blade falls. The world freezes. Widow Capet barely jerks. From out of the basket Apprentice High Executioner Henry pulls Capet's head by the cap and hair and rushes to one corner of the stage to brandish, her eyelids fluttering crazily – is anything witnessed by those eyes? Whereupon Honorine Grosgrain discharges the pistol at the low-down mock-assistant... just as the fulfilled Tanaka rolls aside with ninja skill in a controlled fall from off the scaffold platform. Henry's rushing the head to another corner like a stage conjuror.

Somewhere in the crowd Bingwen Bi dodges into oncoming Tanaka's way, wakizashi foremost. Due to sheer momentum Tanaki spits himself deep through the navel. It's a guilt-free kill. Involuntary suicide. Toshi collapses, breath squealing out of him, writhing, blood spurting from where blood once entered him as a baby.

And a strong hand clamps upon Bingwen Bi's shoulder.

"Four soldiers over here right now – !" Of course the president of the whole event is obeyed.

" – You two get this fancy-dress Man-chu underneath the staging and keep him there. Tie his hands. Other two, carry the dead young Man-chu out of view. No such capers shall ruin the Widow's passing."

And so it is to be, and so it was.

Sanson plants a smart blue shoe of the most exclusively classy newest smuggled patent leather upon Tanaka's messed groin and yanks the wakizashi loose. Abruptly Tanaka lurches and dies. Heart attack perhaps. The execution of dim-wit built-like-a-bull Damiens, who merely pricked the King with a penknife – at which our Sanson was compelled to preside – was far viler and hideously prolonged. Sensibly Sanson cleans the blade upon the ninja's shirt, not so camo now.

The lead ball fired by Mme Honorine misses Tanaka but it does hit a short raggy lad turning to flee the scene since the ex-Queen now lacks a head, therefore all hope of her rescue is gone. The lad doesn't exactly reason this way. Rather, an item in his umwelt becomes nonfunctional non-sense therefore it vanishes.

There's enough impact to shatter his fibula, flooring him. He howls like a dog that doesn't know what to do, and therefore is terrified. Contriving to scramble up, the lad gimps onward gritting his teeth, looking like a snarling terrier, until a citizen swats him flat in case he's rabid. The lad rolls to and fro before going foetal so as to be ignored as just another beggar boy who'll pick pockets no more.

Mason suppresses his instinct to rush away from the scene as if guilty of something. Patiently, "Excusez-moi, je m'excuse – " Softy softly, make self scarcey.

A hand tugs Marie's hair roughly by her cap to pull her neck further forward upon the demilune. She squeals in surprise and affront.

David Mason spends several months of his youth in future Paris, consequently the route to the Luxembourg Gardens needs no help from a HandyHan which he doesn't have.

Nor does Sharma need a guide other than Precious Hairpin even if she's reluctant to leave Revolution Place where her father may still be. However, they had all arranged to escape by TimePod as soon as Tanaka was neutralised. And Maggie Mo swears she saw that happen.

"Maggie, there's something else in here with us."

"I know. Don't try to see it, Raj. Don't try to touch it."

"But *what* – ?"

"It's an aspect of the Scar Pimp. It's half of Sir Percy. *Shhhh*. I hoped – and now I have it! This is far more important than any Toshi Tanaka from Tokyo stranded in time. *Oh Shhhh myself*."

What can Mo mean? She's over-excited as if she just experienced a **eureka**. Calm down, Mags! Yet of a sudden Nineteenth Century Eng Lit don Sharma surprises himself by saying, "We can't see it directly because *our* Umwelt is out of alignment with *its* Umwelt. There's something about this in Coleridge's *Biographia Literaria*." There is not.

"Great thought there, Rajit! That's why I keep you and Mason." Maggie launches the Pod futurewards...

... to arrive in the ballroom of the Randolph Hotel, where all available Guanbo security girls are circling at discreet distances the space which the TimePod may occupy again. They're planets orbiting a gone-away star, they're practitioners of occult martial arts pacing outside a pentacle. The moment that the TimePod manifests, air displaces outward, mussing hairstyles, knocking one Guangdu gal over but nothing fatal.

What a fellow. Psychoshrink, dab hand as a painter, professional photographer with umpteen photos of hysterics.

External speakers on. Colonel Mo uses Mandarin for purposes of record. The lingo collars still oblige for Sharma and Mason. Who knows what the stealthed partial Scar Pimp might be understanding?

"Alert the Institute in Beijing!" Oh yes that's why the use of Mandarin. "Technicians, throw strong netting over the Time Pod. Double the netting over and around the hatch area. Secure the netting tightly."

"Netting from *where*, Colonel?" queries a tech in whites.

"If there's none in the hotel then strip that netting off the Taylorian across the road. The sheer ugliness of using cheap netting instead of printed building wrap sticks in my eye like a grit! All techs except two to assist. Take cutters. Two Security to cover you. Security may use lethal force after one warning in English if anyone obstructs. Super urgent! Go now! Two remaining techs: bring a big cage here as fast as can be. Put a non-tox powder fire extinguisher at the front of the Pod."

That's a very let's say affirmative side of Colonel Mo. If no builders interfere then nobody should get hurt but there's no time to waste.

"Now," murmurs Maggie, "we sit quietly. We look at the floor."

However, Precious Hairpin ventures to murmur, her gaze lowered, "Second-Greatest-Lady, you never truly saw my Father neutralise the Nipponese napist, did you?" Napist rhymes with rapist. "You saw part of the Pimp away from its other part – and you cleverly, with luck, realised what is confirmed here right now."

Sharma squeezes that beloved Han (not Manchu) hand. "Hush, Precious, hush." A shadow from elsewhere shifts within the Pod. Precious Hairpin shivers, so Sharma puts his arm around her.

Maggie murmurs, "I can't expect you to follow this fully, dear, but does Percy Blackeney *understand* his separated situation? Do his separated selves understand? Or do his selves perform automatically and may be *operated* as if by a puppeteer?"

Again, that shadow shifts around its present slice of umwelt.

Another whisper, "And does that part of Percy who is stuck in the past – how, I swear I know not! – along with the part which is here now *remain entangled*? I speak of temporal entanglement!" An exclaimed whisper is still a whisper. "This can be of *extraordinary* value to China – and may even show us how to retrieve your papa, I promise."

"Humbly," whispers Precious Hairpin, "I know nothing about being entangled, except in a net of fowls for the cooking pot. But it occurs to me that you might consider *somnambulism* and *mesmerisation* in order to 'operate' a Percy part?"

"Holy Shit!" whispers Maggie. "That's hypnosis! Baozhai, truly you are the Bee's Knees!" As proud Sharma hears, at least.

"*Mifeng shigai*, eh?" Precious breathes, bewildered.

Presently they hear the modest phut-phut-phut of a Chinese pacifier. More than one *phut* probably signifies firing close overhead as a warning. Maybe one of the builders is a dumb brexist xenophobe. The technicians won't have explained anything to builders; they're too far busy.

Presently-plus, and green plastic netting's being hauled through the ballroom doors to install. So far the shadow – or shadow of a shadow – hasn't shown itself fully, in order to attack for instance.

"All of us ready? Fire extinguisher ready to spray powder? I'm opening the hatch in three-two-one *sān-èr-yī*."

The shadow promptly swoops out into the waiting net. The tech spraying powder reveals the secret kid-size shape. Two arms digging, torso squirming, two legs kicking – all tangled up! Wound around by netting.

"We have it!" cries Maggie. "Where's the cage? Citizens, comrades, guys, WHERE'S THE CAGE? Please Percy the Pimpernel, we only want to talk to you, that's all!"

Our four time travellers crowd at the hatch, inside. No point in going out into all that vomit-green netting. Nauseous colour.

But now the worst happens. Aware of its plight, the half-Percy collapses at once into many mesh-size miniatures – one thinks of scarabs or crabs or fat spiders. These scurry through to liberty, even if this takes some of them twenty or thirty secs. Up drapery they shin, up wallpaper.

"Catch crabs!" Maggie. Crabs are racing to evade capture. Techs launch themselves upon the netting – and squeal. One hero hangs on – and quickly the shadow of substance is inside some big screwtop glass kitchenware, a specimen that darts everywhere within before abruptly ceasing all motion.

"Seal the screwtop with tape," Maggie instructs. "Crittur might try to unscrew from inside like a damn octopus. Guard the jar."

Critturs are at the ceiling, and they're beginning to thin out, so they must have an exit strategy. But be demmed if Sir Percy Blakeney can have ever visited the Randolph, open 70-odd years after Marie's execution. Soon all the bits of the Scar Pimp – bar the one in the jar – have quit the ballroom. Techs hurry to pull the nets away to liberate the time travellers.

"They're rushing along the gutter down Beaumont Street in a crush like football fans," comes a voice from a baronial window flung open.

Mason quickly trundles over to assess. "I bet you they'll lie low in the paddy fields of Worcester College. They probably smell all the mud and water. Question is, can they regain higher functions on their own?"

"*Biggest question* is," from Maggie, "how soon can *we regain* them? Handy-Han, call Thames Valley Police special line."

Code 12339. Colonel Mo requires that all the on-duty force from within 20 kilometres of Carfax Tower throws a cordon around the grounds of Worcester College immediately. Shoulder to shoulder. Dog handlers with their animals included. Protection Group included but without firearms. Buckets to be issued. Repeat Code 12339.

Affirm Marm, thank you Ma'am. May I say personally what an honour –

Marmy smarmy.

P recious Hairpin's first sight of modernity is of the noon airport bus departing from outside the Randolph – a humble palace – towards Brize Norton International Airport. But no passengers of that bus will board their flights because police cars are already converging from patrols in order to start cordoning. A spotter helicopter is overhead, spotting it knows not what yet. A giant dragonfly that chatters. The Ashmolean Museum across the road is adequately large and classical to belong in the Paris of Precious. Infrequent shiny small coaches have no horses pulling them.

"Can the persons inside that yellow coach be propelling it so fast with their feet, wearing clogs?" asks Precious.

Mollie Mo is saying to one of her Guoanbu security women, "I need to supervise from close by, but also *comfortably*, not an incident field tent in the Gloucester Green car park. I've just been this close to the guillotine in Paris during the Terror." She pulls off her tricoleur cockade and tosses it upon the pavement. She talks in Guangdongese but all those with lingo collars catch this, except for Precious Hairpin who hasn't a collar. What need? Precious already speaks Mandarin and French and English. Best Japanese Collars don't grow on trees. Hurry up, Chi-Tech! You already made all the trains run on time at super high speed with kids' comic book fun interiors to entertain passengers when the landscape moves too fast to see.

"I say," says Mason, drawing alongside Maggie, "Paddyfields just around the corner in Hythe Bridge Street is tops for dimsum lunch. You'll remember us all meeting there before we extracted Fibonacci."

"*Who?* Oh yes! Of course I remember the restaurant. Professor Quinan Lin of Beijing was there, for one thing." To the security woman: "Chui, sprint ahead and commandeer the Paddyfields place. Full use and cooperation, usual compensation. Inform Police."

> "We can't see it directly because *our* Umwelt is out of alignment with *its* Umwelt. There's something about this in Coleridge's *Biographia Literaria*."

Maggie adds in English or French or Mandarin, "That'll let our Precious Hairpin experience something familiar, a treat to settle her." In her blue-uniformed chevroned-cuffed uniform, Colonel Mo gloats somewhat to herself:

"Quantum entanglement of partial persons in time! Oh wow. Self-congratulations. Beijing will be top happy."

Another Guangbo Gal catches up and Maggie tells her, "The Police should all be issued with rubber boots and hundreds of kids' bamboo fishing nets as well as buckets – make those pails. And strong surgical gloves. Tell the Assistant Chief Constable to meet me inside Paddyfields for briefing the moment she gets here. Tonia Taylor. We have hours of light yet."

So now they arrive at the Chinese restaurant where the fire alarm is still shrilling while the last few customers hurry out, receiving on the way a set meal dinner voucher from security officer Chui. Thus positive and negative are balanced, yin and yang.

"Dim sum dumplings coming up, coming up, My fair la-dy!" Prof Mason rejoices. Once more Maggie Mo's expense account provides.

Ian Watson is a long-standing judge of the Aeon Award.

Pandora's Mailbag

Tod J. McCaffrey

There is always a price of admission. Once paid, everything in The Deadman's Silence is free.

I was at the bar. Drinking water.

Footsteps from behind alerted me as she stepped close. I looked up hopefully. She looked down as she sat herself, her lips twisting humorously. Fat chance. She didn't have to say the words. She never did.

Mack – Mackenzie Russell – had known me for a while now. Not a long time, no one knew me for a long time, but a while.

Once again, I cursed my luck. I looked soulfully up at her and fingered my drink.

"Whiskey," Mack said to the unseen bartender, giving me a thoughtful look. "Make it a double."

"What?" I cried in surprise. "Mack, that's jolly decent of you."

Her lips twitched upwards as the barman slid the drink across to her and, with a wink, she tipped it down her throat.

She wiped her lips and shook her head, frowning at the empty glass. "Nope, let's try vodka."

"I don't like vodka," I told her.

"It's not for you," Mack said.

"You're having *another*?" I cried in surprise. A glass of clear liquid slid across the bar and Mack downed it, too, in one quick gulp. "But Mack – you don't drink!"

She tapped her empty glass on the table and wiggled a finger to the barperson for a refill.

"I do now." She toyed with the new drink before downing it, as well, and signaling for yet another. She looked down at me. "I might have a job for you."

"What's in it for me?" I asked in my damnably high piping voice. I signaled the barman, saying, "I'll have what she's having."

A large glass of water was slid my way and I sighed. This place has rules – I'd die of thirst before they served me alcohol. A long, long time ago, I'd asked who was to know but never got an answer. It was one in a long, long line of questions for which I'd got no answers.

In here, asking questions is never a good idea. The petrified cat in the front hall is testimony to that. It and the statues dotted around the various rooms and lounges. From their horrified expressions, I had a pretty good idea how they got here – and who made them.

I also had a good guess how Mack had found this place. Me? I was one of the founding members.

Fountain of Youth, what a fucking stupid idea! I was older back then and not as smart.

Now? Now I am forever ten.

Which makes looking at someone like Mack more than a little irritating. Sea-green eyes, tall, very tall, thin, wiry, lithe, curly blond hair – even an old Indian like me could see something in her.

And... something more. Whatever it was that brought her into the Deadman's Silence. This place. I could see it around her eyes. I saw it now, even after her fourth double shot.

This is a place where you don't ask questions because the answers might kill you. So I'd never quite gotten around to asking Mack why she still came.

She'd arrived as a youngster in her early teens. Exactly what had brought her here, what had got her beyond the petrified cat, I've never quite discovered. My guess? The same thing that gets most pretty girls to leave their home and never go back.

"I'll have another," Mack said, raising her empty glass to the barman. It disappeared when she set it down and a fresh glass took its place. She looked down at me. "Are you interested?"

"Tell me."

Mack downed the shot, banged the bar for another and said, "You've got to get me home."

"Okay." I didn't know where she lived – she'd have to tell me. That was worth something by itself.

She knew she could trust me. I didn't just *look* ten years old, dammit.

"I was at the Home," Mack said, fingering her fresh drink and eyeing its contents.

I said nothing.

"Dooley passed," she said. "But not before he handed me this." She reached into the purse hanging from her shoulder and slid a letter across the bar to me.

There was no postmark, no return address. The letter was very old, yellowed, and frazzled. The address read:
Martin Dooley
Sunny Valley Retirement Home
Syosset, New York
November 23rd, 2014

I frowned at the date. That was today. I squinted at the envelope – the lettering of the address and the date matched, they were equally as old.

"Open it."

I opened the envelope and took out a single piece of paper. It read: 5:43 p.m.

I glanced up at Mack. Her jaw tightened; she drained her shot, slamming it down on the bar for a refill.

"That's when he died?"

"To the second," she said.

"Voodoo? Shaman?" I asked. I raised the envelope to my nose and sniffed it. Some gifts never die, no matter how old you are – I could smell age, cologne, dust – but no magic.

"He asked for me," Mack said, downing the new drink and rapping for another. "I was doing a piece on the last of the World War Two vets, so he'd heard."

"He wasn't on your list?"

"He wouldn't have anything to do with me," Mack said. "Not until today." She closed her eyes.

I frowned, took a long drink of my water and then sighed. I raised a hand toward her. "May I?"

She opened her eyes briefly then nodded, closing them again, putting her left hand, palm up, open, on the table.

Gingerly, I put my right hand on top of it, closed my eyes and let her memories fall into me.

"**M**ista Dooley wants to see you, Miss," Mrs. Johnson said as I went into the lobby of the old folk's home that morning.

"Where is he?" I asked, hiding my surprise at both the news and its messenger. Mrs. Johnson hadn't said one kind word to me in the two weeks since I'd first arrived. She'd sniff when I arrived and only motion directions when I asked. I was too young, too pretty to be here, in her opinion. I got the notion she thought I

In here, asking questions is never a good idea. The petrified cat in the front hall is testimony to that.

was some sort of gold-digger.

"He's in the Sun Room, Miss," Mrs. Johnson said, gesturing as though she was directing me there for the first time.

"Mr. Madison was expecting me…"

"Mr. Madison left us last night," Mrs. Johnson said in a steady voice.

My breath caught and I gave her a jerky nod. "Did he pass in his sleep?"

"He died with a horrible scream and a look like Satan himself had come for him," Mrs. Johnson said with a righteous look on her face. She leaned over the counter toward me. "Maybe he had amends to make."

Amends. Meaning: cavorting with me.

"Mr. Dooley was the last one with him," Mrs. Johnson said, gesturing toward the Sun Room once more.

"Okay," I said, moving off. If I'd stayed much longer, Mrs. Johnson would have… I shook the thought out of my head; it was better that way.

Mr. Dooley was instantly recognizable. He'd been on my short list, especially given his age and experience. He'd been with the 1st Infantry Division from North Africa through to V-E Day; one of the very few combat infantrymen to have survived the war whole and stay sane.

He was still cogent, nearly a hundred years later. He was an excellent subject.

"Mr. Dooley?" I said as I approached him. He was in a wheelchair like so many and sat slumped, facing the sun but still in the shade.

There was a blanket over his legs. On top of the blanket was something else. Yellowed paper. He lifted it up when he saw me.

"The last one," he said in an old, old croaky voice. I could barely hear him. With a glance for permission, I grabbed one of the visitor chairs – a cheap office chair – and pulled it in front of him.

"The last one of what, sir?" I said. So many of them reacted well to the honorific.

"'Sir'? I worked for my living!" Mr. Dooley croaked in reply.

"Sorry," I said, but I could tell that he was secretly pleased.

"No," he said, shaking his head just a bit, "I s'pose you can say it." He glanced over at me. "You sure is pretty, you know."

Yeah, I knew. I forced myself to recognize that he was trying to be polite: gallant. "Thank you."

His old eyes caught mine and he held them for a long moment before dropping them once more to his lap.

"Someone hurt you," he said in a barely audible croak. He lifted his head again. "Sorry."

I waved that away. "You didn't do it."

"Shouldn't have been done," he said, shaking his head.

"You wanted to see me, sir?" I asked, fearing that he'd get lost in his thoughts.

"This is the last," he said again, hefting the object in his lap. It was an envelope. He pushed it toward me. "You open it."

I took the envelope and glanced at it. Then I took a longer look.

Mr. Dooley's dry chuckle distracted me.

"Gave Madison his yesterday," Dooley said. "Only thing that matters is the time." He shook his head, his eyes going wide. "I've got to have enough time."

"Sir?" I was lost. Gave Mr. Madison what?

"Open it!" Mr. Dooley ordered, his voice croaking. "Don't dawdle, child!" To himself he muttered, "Don't have no respect these days. Too rushed, never stop to think."

I ignored that, having heard it constantly from the retirees, and carefully opened the envelope. There was a single sheet of paper inside, just as old. Carefully, I unfolded it. There was only a time written in the center of the paper: 5:43 p.m.

"What's it say?" Mr. Dooley demanded, feebly waving at the paper. When I didn't answer immediately, he raised his voice, "Well, ain't got all day, what's it say?"

"It's says five forty-three p.m.," I told him, passing the letter back to him.

"Hmmph!" He said, dropping the paper on the floor, as though it were unimportant. "What's the time?" I looked at him in confusion. "What's the time now, girl?"

I glanced around and found the large clock on the wall behind him. "It's a bit after noon. Twelve twenty."

"That's enough," he said to himself. He nodded his head once. "Yes, that should be enough," he said to himself. He looked up at me, his eyes bright. "You said you wanted to talk to me?" I nodded. "Well, you've got your chance. But first, let me tell you."

I reached into my purse and pulled out my voice recorder and notepad.

"Can I record this?"

"Sure," he said with a wave of his hand.

I smiled at him and turned the recorder on. "I'm talking with Mr. Martin Dooley, this is November twenty-third, two thousand and fourteen and the time is twelve twenty-one. Mr. Dooley, for the recorder, do you consent to being recorded?"

"Don't dawdle, girl, I haven't got all day!"

"Mr. Dooley," I said in a soothing tone, "I just need your permission."

"Sure, sure!" he said, waving his hand. "Do what you need."

"Thank you," I said, leaning closer toward him. "Now, sir, you said you have something you wanted to tell me?"

"Got a job, too, if you're strong enough," Mr. Dooley replied. "You find it, you do what you want with it."

"Sir?"

"I was in the war," Martin Dooley said. "I was in the worst of it, in the infantry all the way to V-E day."

I nodded politely.

He gestured to the letter in his lap. "Took these with me, too, after they killed Sarge –"

"Who would be?"

"Ain't no time," Mr. Dooley replied. "Took 'em on when he was killed just like he took 'em on after the lieutenant." He glanced down at his lap. "This is the last one we took. The last one out of the bag." He snorted, shaking his head. "Wish we'd never laid our eyes on that damned bag.

"Shoulda known better, too," he said to himself. He glanced up at me. "You know about El Guettar?"

"The battle?" I knew a fair bit: I'd studied it up just in the hope of being able to talk to Mr. Dooley about it.

"The worst battle of the war," Dooley said with a sigh. "After it, nothing was hard –" he looked into my eyes "– and killing Germans was easy."

He said it as so many had said it before him – with a hint of apology and an iron resolve.

For a long while he was silent, lost in bitter memories.

"That's where we found it," he said finally.

"Sir?"

"The bag," Dooley said. He shook his head from side to side. "'Can't remember quite who found it but we handed it to the LT."

I waited.

"The lieutenant was all for throwing it away. But it had stuff in it and when he opened it, he pulled out a stack of letters.

"The LT swore when he looked at the first one." Dooley pursed his lips, looking ready to spit. "Must've made too much noise because a sniper nailed him just then.

"We all looked around and some of us started firing blindly," Dooley continued. "We were pissed – pardon – because that LT, he wasn't so bad and now we'd have to break in another.

"Sarge pulled the bag away from the LT, pushed it out of sight – it was white, you see, easy for a sniper to mark – and then we all moved back," Dooley said. He shook his head. "Somehow Sarge held onto some of the letters.

"We were stuck there until dark and then we pulled back, found the CO and let him know the LT was dead." Mr. Dooley pursed his lips once more and shook his head. "The CO swore when he heard how the LT had died. 'Damn fool! Damn fool!' he said." He shook his head again. "We could tell that he liked the LT, too, 'cuz he said 'damn fool' twice.

"The battle sort of ended the next day and we managed to get back to the LT," Dooley continued. "We figured to get him a proper burial. Some of the letters were still there, of course." He shook his head. "I don't know where the bag went."

I waited and waited. "Mr. Dooley?"

"Sorry," he roused himself, his eyes wet with unshed tears. "The letter in the LT's hand – Sarge pulled it away from him, his whole body was stiff, you know – and when he read it he swore, just like the LT.

"I'd been rifling through the letters and I stopped. 'Sarge, there's one here for you!' I told him. "Well, he turned bright white and I looked at him in wonder. He passed me the LT's letter.

"It was addressed to the LT," Dooley said, shaking his head. "It was addressed: Lieutenant Roscoe B. Buchanan, El Guettar, March 23, 1943. The day he was killed." He paused for a moment, then gestured to the letter in his lap. "And the letter had a time on it: 12:10 a.m. That was the time the LT died."

"Sarge's envelope read 'Sergeant Anson Letheridge, Hill 232, May 6th, 1943.'" Mr. Dooley shook his head. "There were a lot of letters with that date on them." He cocked his head at me. "You understand now what the letters mean?"

"Did your sergeant die on May 6th at Hill 232?"

Mr. Dooley snorted. "Him and most of the battalion. Wasn't much more than thirty of us left after that." He was quiet for a long moment. "Later, I heard that General Allen had ordered the attack just 'cuz he wanted a fight." He snorted. "Damn fool. He lost his son in 'Nam years later." Dooley sighed. "I had a letter for that, too."

"How many letters did you have?"

"Too many!" He swore. He made a face. "Did you know I was married?"

I shook my head.

"By then I'd put all the letters away, up in the attic," he said. "I didn't want to look at them anymore." He made a face. "Only my wife, she was looking for something in the attic. And she found the letters. There was one for her.

"We were just newly married, it was after the war and she was my childhood sweetheart," Mr. Dooley said in a sad, tired voice. "She found the letter and we argued. She ran away, took the car – some drunk hit her head on the next day. Her letter burned with her... but I'll bet it had the right time inside."

"I see," I told him. "But that's the last letter, what do you want from me?"

"It's the last letter we *took*, Miss," Mr. Dooley said, shaking his head. "But there's a whole bag back there, somewhere in Tunisia."

"And you want me to find it?"

"I want you to destroy it," Mr. Dooley said, his voice croaking. "Do you know how hard it's been, dealing with all those letters?" He shook his head. "No one should have to bear that burden. No one should have to know when their wife is going to die. Or their son. Or their President."

"President?"

"There was one addressed to John Fitzgerald Kennedy, November 23rd, 1963," Mr. Dooley said. "I stuck it in an envelope and mailed it to the White House. I don't know if they even opened it." He stopped for a moment. "'Spose it wouldn't have mattered anyway."

Mack pulled her hand out from under mine. Tears were flowing down her cheeks.

"I stayed with him until it was time," she said to me, draining yet another shot and banging on the bar for a refill.

"He died on time?" I repeated my earlier question because I needed to know.

"To the second."

"It could have been that he was so convinced –"

"And his wife? The lieutenant who didn't have time to react?"

I was silent for a long while. "Why did you tell me?"

Mack drained her new glass in one gulp and pushed herself away from the table, wobbling slightly.

"Help me home."

I got up and stood beside her. She leaned down and put an arm over my shoulder. I led her out of the bar, past the petrified cat, up the stairs and into the misty night.

She directed me turn by turn and I guided her home. I was surprised to discover that she lived only a few blocks

"Only thing that matters is the time." He shook his head, his eyes going wide. "I've got to have enough time."

away in a nice building complete with doorman. The doorman knew her and gave me a strange look until she said, "He's with me, George, it's okay."

"Miss?" George had detected the alcohol on his breath.

"Seeing-eye-child," I told him, tugging her up the steps and into the lobby.

"Apartment 314," she said. She patted her purse which hung off her shoulder on my side. It had been chafing against me the whole way. "Keys in there."

With a frown, I rooted around and pulled out a large set of keys. We got on the elevator and I propped her up against the wall. When the bell chimed and the doors opened, I had to wake her up. She'd been snoring softly.

I got her inside her apartment with some difficulty.

"Do you want me to make some coffee?"

"Bed, sleep," she replied, waving a hand toward a doorway. I guided her there and sat her on the bed. She tried to toe off her shoes but failed. I pulled them off for her.

"You need water or you'll feel worse in the morning," I told her.

"Can't feel worse," she said in a slurred voice. She flopped her head on the bed.

For a long while I looked at her, seeing the features that had grown out of her teenage face into this new almost grown-up. She was snoring again, her head at an awkward angle.

I sighed and looked around. In a chest of drawers, I found some pajamas.

"I'm going to get you into bed," I said to her snoring self. It was awkward and hard, given my size, but I got her out of her clothes, into her pajamas, and under the covers.

She roused as I positioned the pillow under her head. She patted the bed beside her. "Stay."

"Mack..."

She opened her eyes and pierced me with them. "Please?" I hesitated. "You can go in the morning."

"Go where?"

"Tunisia," she said like it was obvious. "Find the bag, see if you've got a letter." She patted the bed again. "Tonight, be my little brother." She shivered. "My back's cold."

I could not say no to her. I changed, got in beside her and turned my back to hers. She scooted herself against me.

Maybe I would go in the morning and find the bag. Maybe not. For me, it wouldn't matter. There would be no envelope for me. That wasn't why Mack wanted me to go. She wanted me to find her envelope, to find it and keep it safe, to keep her from knowing. She wanted to tie me to her just as she was tying me to her now, so that there would be someone – some family, no matter how strange – to be there with her when she took her last breath. She could trust me, of course. It was her gift. The gift that let her share memories just by touching. Somehow that gift had bought her entry into The Deadman's Silence. With Dooley, she'd earned it twice.

Me? I had drunk from the Fountain of Youth. I would never die. Mack would age, wither, turn querulous like Private Dooley, and, one day, die.

And I would still be ten.

Todd McCaffrey writes science fiction and fantasy, most recently *L.A. Witch: The Last Dragon*.

Step Right up
Roelof Goudriaan

"You were the first one out of bed that day." I stop ten words into my letter, hating my clumsy beginning. *Of course you were first.* Finn Ferguson, the county's number one insurance agent, the archetype of self-made success: you use 'first' as your middle name. How *inadequate* you'd find the way I express myself.

That thought brings me the adrenaline to continue my letter.

I was still solidly asleep when the clock radio went off at a quarter past six. The newscaster's voice was even shriller than the loudspeaker usually managed. "Across the country, gigantic spheres are appearing in the sky! All contact with Leitrim and Sligo has been lost. The Army and Air Corps are ..." Groggily, I nearly fell getting out of bed, my foot caught in the sheets. "Are the Russians invading? For the latest, over to – "

Outside, a noise was swelling to a thunderous din. With a few stumbling steps I sought your support. As we were standing there, the window frame of our bedroom disappeared with a loud sucking pop, and the hole peeled open further until the entire wall was gone, within mere split seconds.

Naked in your arms, mouth agape and wide-eyed, I looked through the hole into the street. Hundreds of metallically gleaming squid-like creatures slithered through swirling dust and sand. Some only fist-sized, others with body bags bigger than a bus, were sliding over and along the facades on the other side of our street, their tentacles moving faster than my eyes could follow. Dust was swept up everywhere. In the middle of the street I noticed three figures who were standing inside a bubble where the dust storm did not penetrate. They were wearing ridiculous outfits – the nearest sported a red afro wig, yellow-and-red plaid slacks and wacky shoes, and to his right stood a woman in a glittery silver bikini and a feather headdress. The third wore tight-fitting red velvet trousers and a tailcoat, and a black top hat. The clown and the glittergirl were conducting fervently with their arms, the man in the top hat was cracking a whip. In the street, the squid-like figures grabbed everything in sight with their tentacles. They swallowed objects many times larger than themselves into their body bags. Within thirty seconds, they had gobbled the lampposts and parked cars in the street, and our neighbours' facades across the street were by now gone, too.

Your arm fell off my shoulders. I looked aside. I had never seen you like this. Three years ago you had managed to charm me, though you were more dead than alive at the time, as I was nursing you in the ICU ward. You'd whispered you were too much of a gentleman to hit Lady Death, but that it might help if I could make Her a bit jealous by kissing you on the cheek. But now, you gawked at the apocalypse outside with blindly staring eyes, crouched in your pajamas like a whipped dog.

The air raid siren sounded from the center of town. The bedroom floor creaked. The dust was around everywhere and made my eyes water. I pushed my panic down to my toes – months of therapist visits finally paid off. "We must get out of here!" I screamed, right into your ear so you might hear me over the roaring noise. When you didn't respond, I slapped your cheek hard. You jerked back, then nodded. You fled through the door to the stairwell without looking back, though I noticed that you did find time to snatch your watch from the chair as you passed.

We were only half way down the stairs when the steps were snatched away from below us. We tumbled down screaming for a heartbeat, until suction cups caught us from our free fall and released us into the pit where our house had stood just a minute ago. A piece of debris scratched my head just above my ear. The unexpected pain made me scream, my first sound since I got up. I kept screaming for minutes, as if a spark had detonated a powder keg inside me.

We were laying on damp earth. The basement walls had all disappeared, even the utility pipes had been hijacked from the ground. Side by side, me still naked, half raised on my elbows, we stared into the dust. Then the clown appeared at the edge of the well. He made obeisance to us. His eyes had yellow pupils, I saw now, cleaved by narrow black slits. "Step right up, folks!" he squeaked, with the falsetto of a Marilyn Manson doing a Betty Boop voice-over. "Step *right* up!"

The clown threw his red wig in the air. My eyes unwittingly followed that wig, up and impossibly further up until it disappeared from view. When I forced my gaze down again, I saw that the figure had donned a new set of clothes, jeans and a pink T-shirt that I recognized as mine by the F*CK TR*CKERS slogan On his bald head he wore a baseball cap, a little slanted the way I like to do during a wild night out. And the bastard had even stolen that posh wrist watch you'd received during the best-insurer-of the-year award affair!

A kraken at least twenty feet tall slithered past, swinging its tentacles. The monster blared a continuous three-tone. We tried to protect our eardrums with our hands, but the scream pierced past our fingers. The clown turned, tapped the baseball cap, and disappeared from view.

The siren wail faded quickly, and moments later the only sound I heard was the sobbing of some neighbours.

You carefully looked for a hold and pulled yourself up at a ledge. When peeking over the edge of the pit, you almost fell down again. I felt a spat of rain. The dust began to settle, but this hole would soon become a muddy, slippery mess. The cold rippled through my naked body. I shivered and followed you up.

Our house wasn't the only object that had been sucked away. The whole road was gone. There were a few wagons and donkeys, blades of grass, sand and clay, that's all. I could see some trees in the distance – the neighbourhood park? But as far as I my eyes could see, not a single structure had survived.

In the distance hovered one of the metal spheres that the newscaster had mentioned. A shiny red ball, hanging in the air without any support or engine noise. From all directions teeming masses moved towards the sphere. Living tsunamis they looked like, which were sucked up from above and disappeared into the sphere. That silver pencil, was that a LUAS? How big was that sphere? Two hundred meters? Three hundred? I had no idea, the emptied landscape offered too little to hold on to.

The writhing mass started to dwindle. Before I could ask you anything, the orb had absorbed the last stragglers, and now floated playfully up like a red balloon, higher and higher, until it suddenly disappeared. A gust of wind swept across the land.

"There's one of those weird wagons in front of our house too, Finn," I said, pointing to the other side of the pit which had been our home, "and a donkey."

"Let's check it out," you said grimly. "It's not like we have a fecking choice."

Of course I followed you. Covering my breasts and pubic hair as best I could with my hands, I was running toward the wagon in search of shelter. Here and there other people appeared, as dazed and naked as I was. I saw our neighbours crawl out of their basement. I was relieved – I liked them – but I didn't dare wave.

The sides of the wagon were painted in a brick red. The back of the wagon turned out to have a door. " Windows, with shutters?" I said surprised. "A trailer?" You paid me no attention, you were too indignant seeing the number plate which had been screwed underneath the door. "That's *my* license plate!" you shouted. "From *my* Tesla Imperator!"

"See if we can get in," I nudged you. "I'm dying from the rain and cold. We need clothes, now!"

The interior of the trailer had turned your shock into chilly despair. "Like I stepped right into the Wanderly Wagon!" you complained. "Decrepit junk, the lot!" I noticed a trundle bed, a cooking pot, some cutlery and plates, and for both of us – oh, what luck! – a set of clothes. I immediately put on the red jacket with brass uniform buttons that lay on the bed, and the tight red miniskirt that came with it. The bellhop hat was especially cute. "Look at me, Finn!" I said spinning around. "I look like that lobby boy in The Grand Budapest Hotel, remember that movie?" You kept quiet. The glittery heels also fit me perfectly, better than any pair I'd ever bought.

You had at first flatly refused to put on the only other set of clothes in the trailer, even after the rain had stopped. "A fool's suit, come on!" But after fifteen minutes' sulking in the draughty caravan, you finally came out, shuffling and looking at the ground. I heard you before I saw you from the corner of my eye, but I didn't want to leave the circle in which our neighbours were sitting. We had been comforting each other, given each other courage with every embrace. Something like that really helps, I felt a lot better by now.

Your jester costume fit you just fine. But you hated it, that was the first thing you brought up when joining us. The colorful red, green and yellow patches, and especially the bells that were attached all over your suit, even on the top of your green curling shoes. You resolutely refused to put on the jester's hood, fastened seamlessly to the collar of your suit. The jingling hoodie dangled on your back.

Our neighbour Darragh, a mid-twenty-something who had been living across the street, wore knee-high boots and a leopard skin which accentuated the muscles in his arms and legs. His equally muscular and even taller partner Maxim wore a brown leather trapper outfit and moccasins. He also wore a gun belt with two pistols.

"Our first concern is to get enough food, to be able to protect ourselves from gangs, and most importantly, fresh water. Because the water mains have disappeared like everything else," gestured Darragh. "Survival, folks, that takes precedence over everything else." The al-Lahayis of number 15 and the Baker family of number 19 nodded their agreement.

"Why don't we just wait a few hours for the Red Cross to arrive?" you objected. "Or the army? They must have been mobilized a good while ago, don't you think?"

Darragh cast a pitying glance at you. "You're listening to the wrong newscast, neighbour. Or you're getting up too late. I've been following the entire invasion since 5 am. What happened here has happened everywhere! And the military did already show up! With tanks and fighter jets!"

"Well then," you said indignantly. "That should get us some results, shouldn't it?"

"Oh yes," Maxim said mockingly. He drew his two pistols, pointed them at you. "To be precise, THIS!" He shot. You screamed. From Maxim's right pistol, a trickle of water hit you right in the face. Sputtering, you fell backwards, on the ground. The second gun showered you with flowers.

"Daisies, confetti, water, that's all they could fire. Like second-rate clowns from a third-rate circus," Maxim said bitterly.

"Hey, Max!" I stomped forward, swallowing because I was a head shorter than the bodybuilder, but I had to protect you as you would no doubt protect me. So I pressed an index finger to Maxim's chest and looked way up into his eyes in my undersized fury. "We are all in shock and full of frustration. But will you please not take that out on the others? This is of no use to anyone!"

Maxim took a step back. His shoulders slumped, his pistols were dangling down in cramped hands, and the giant of a man looked close to crying. I had already removed my finger, and now I embraced him. You scrambled to your feet. Maxim's pistols continued to spew their circus munitions, but it now only hit the ground around our feet, where a rapidly growing pool of petaled water formed.

"Um, excuse me, but is the water which that gun is spraying fresh?" eleven-year-old Lina al-Lahayi broke the silence. "Because if it somehow keeps spraying without emptying, at least we've solved our water shortage problems."

That night you were tossing incessantly. After a while you even got up and I heard a dull thud, after which you started cursing in muffled tones. "How can I sell insurances like this," you sobbed when you got back inside. "Never ask a fool to buy something from another fool! Have I become a champion salesman to be served off as the laughingstock of the fecking whole of Waterford?"

"The morning light will bring counsel, my dear," I consoled, taking your right hand in my hands and dabbing with a damp cloth at the pain.

The rest of the night you spent lying in my arms. I felt the restrained jerk of every sob you tried to hide from me.

The next morning Quintin had set out on a voyage of discovery. He had been given a penny-farthing along with his bear suit, and the previous day he had taught himself the hard way to keep his balance on top of the large front wheel. Nevertheless, even that kind of a bicycle was a lot faster than a trip on foot or with one of the donkeys they had been gifted.

The rest of us rearranged our trailers into a big circle in front of the former neighbourhood park. The trees and shrubs gave us shelter from the wind and the overwhelming emptiness of the landscape. When you looked at the trees, you could even pretend for just a moment that the world was more or less normal.

The kids had embraced their circus costumes, and were out and about all day like tumbling acrobats, contortionists and juggling ballerinas. They got better at it every hour. It's amazing how quickly children learn! An old neighbour had collapsed in the afternoon under all the uncertainty, and now was lying down exhausted in her trailer. Quintin's wife Louise and I took turns to see if we could help with anything.

Over the course of the day, people started seeking me out more and more often when they were trying to solve a practical problem or just needed to be cheered up. "How nice to have you with us, Pauline," Tina Baker from number nineteen said after one of our talks, and gave me a hug. That seemed to inspire you to also make an effort to get to know the neighbours better. I was beginning to hope that you too had begun to accept this bewildering world.

At nightfall, most of us were sitting around the firewood campfire we had built together. We were all waiting for Quintin's return. We had just finished our evening meal. Sean from number 13, a beanpole of a teenager in a tailcoat and striped trousers, had pulled rabbit after rabbit out of his top hat, and Darragh had killed and skinned them out of sight of the children. "I didn't know I'd be so good at that," he muttered in a surprised tone when he returned with the five skinned rabbits.

We drank tea from steaming mugs that Louise and I had been handing round. "I have to take care of my three children," Louise laughed, "so why not take care of my neighbours?" The lace-up jacket and floral apron she wore enhanced her maternal appearance. I also liked to stay busy: it stopped me from worrying about our situation.

Maxim jumped up. "Quintin has returned!" he shouted. He seemed to be getting eagle-eyed. A bit later, all of us saw a furry shape on a high-wheel bicycle jerking over the bumpy dust path.

We cheered Quintin as he cycled the last fifty metres. As soon as he'd gotten down, Louise pulled up his bear hood and gave him a huge smack on the mouth. Quintin beamed. "I've travelled sixty kilometers today," he cried, looking around the circle that had gathered around him, "and that's quite a feat on that bicycle!" He petted the penny-farthing affectionately. "It's the same everywhere. Everyone looks the way we do. I've seen two other bears, ringmasters, knife throwers, lions and zebra-suited people, people with moving tattoos, even two sisters stuck to each other at the hips like conjoined twins. Lots of clowns, a few jesters ... and they just put their hoods on, Finn, really!" He tugged at your hood with a smile. You grimaced in response.

"Blackfriars has disappeared, the cathedrals... The station is gone. Cars, radios, computers, roads ... – the lot." He sighed. Louise crept closer to him.

"But," he looked up, "a bearded woman from Dunmore East told me that she had heard a rumour about a living cannonball who'd seen a huge circus tent near Hook Head. Red-and-white tarpaulin and waving flags, he said, at the end of the only paved road in the wide area – feck, perhaps the only one in the country!"

That evening, the circus tent was the only topic the circle of people around the campfire talked about. The al-Lahayis, the Bakers, everyone had questions they wanted to ask Quintin.

"I'm exhausted," Quintin said a few hours later. "Dear people, I'll see you tomorrow." Arm in arm with Louise, they walked to their trailer, surrounded by their children.

You noticed that Quintin had put on his bear head again. "That's not normal, Pauline," you whispered. "That is downright disturbing."

I wasn't sure what to believe. You like to exaggerate and a lot, I've always known that. But you weren't completely wrong either.

The next morning you woke up next to me, startled and wide-eyed. I smiled. "Cozy, that crib," I said, and rubbed my hips against you suggestively. When you didn't allow yourself to respond, I got out of bed, donned my bellhop uniform, and performed a teasing pirouette before leaving our trailer.

The sun was still low on the horizon, but the camp was already full of movement. The water in the pot was bubbling, and Louise was busy at work. Sean upended gallons of barley from his magician's hat into the cooking pot, then fetched a dozen croissants with cheese and ham out of that same hat. "Yesterday I could only find rabbits in that hat," he beamed, "but today almost everything seems to work for me."

I helped Louise with breakfast again, stacking porridge bowls in my hands. "Pauline girl, you seem more agile every day," she smiled at me. Still, she seemed a bit depressed.

Quintin sat quietly on the floor next to Louise, and after Louise had scooped out the last gruel, he licked the pot. When most our bowls started to get empty, Louise cleared her throat and said, "Quintin and I have decided we're going. To the Head. Looking for the circus, I mean." She twisted with her foot. "But we don't want to leave anyone behind. Come with us, dear neighbours! The more the merrier."

She took a step toward her trailer, turned around. "We'll leave when the sun has reached its zenith. "

Throughout the circle, couples and families started discussing among themselves.

"Louise is right," I said as you and I retreated to our trailer. "What happened? What's next? Here we'll never find an answer to our questions, Finn. We'll have to search to find them!"

"But dear," you cried, "what makes you think we're going to find it elsewhere? The only hold we have is here. Here we can survive. We have to be patient. It's a matter of days before the Red Cross comes, or the Americans, or…" You couldn't come up with another off-the-cuff saviour, and that frustrated you. "Well, someone! There are so many aid organizations with infinitely more resources and capabilities than we have! Do you think *we're* going to save the world," you waved your arms around you in the cramped space, "a jester and a bellhop in a donkey wagon?" Your fool's bells were taking up the sound of your voice and kept jingling until I could no longer tell them apart.

"Oh, Finn!" I stamped on the plank floor and twirled around on my heels. I slammed the door open and stormed out. "Chicken!" I cried. It infuriated me that

The figure had donned jeans and a pink T-shirt that I recognized as mine by the F*CK TR*CKERS slogan.

you were blinded by uncertainty, that you didn't want to see what we had to gain.

But maybe I had a lot more to gain than you…

An hour later I came back to the trailer, where you were curled up on the bed. "We belong together, you and I, Finn," I said softly. "We go'll there with the two of us, or we stay here with the two of us. I trust you."

You turned to me. Eyes wide with astonishment you told me, "What have I done to deserve you?" That moment I recognized you again, Finn, as my suitor from way back.

Quintin returned from the makeshift meadow in the old neighbourhood park. The donkey next to him seemed to be guided by Quintin's soothing humming noises. He just held rein loosely in one. With quiet gestures he harnassed the donkey in front of their trailer, much more smoothly than you would expect from a man in a bear suit.

Louise and I embraced as if the end of time had come. Sniffling, we traded good advice and wished each other the world.

Half an hour later, five of the trailers left the camp. Mr. Baker played "What A Wonderful World" on his trumpet from the box of his wagon, while his wife in her sequined corset dress drove the donkey and tipped her top hat as a salute. Louise was waving her handkerchief the entire time, and I waved back until long after the procession of trailers had disappeared from sight.

You helped, as silently as the others, to regroup the eight remaining trailers in a smaller circle.

That evening, Maxim helped me build the campfire, and the al-Lahayi children came and helped with chores. You helped me with the provisions that Sean had given us out of his hat. We finally broke free of the feeling of being stragglers now that we had some mugs of steaming tea in our hands.

"Come and see, everyone!" the bass voice of Rayan al-Lahayi interrupted us. You took my hand and we hurried with our neighbours toward Rayan's voice. A few stumbled, for the moon and stars barely reached through the thick cloud cover this night and darkness was almost total.

But in that darkness, far away, in the direction of the Head, we could see a faint glow in the sky. Until two days ago, none of us would have paid any attention to such a dim source of light, had we even discovered it among the lights with which our town drowned out the night. But tonight we experienced that diffuse, warm glow like a new Pharos of Alexandria.

"That's *not* the fecking lighthouse," Maxim cursed, breaking the silence.

Darragh looked as awestruck as we all. "Quintin, Louise and the others must have arrived there already. I can imagine it all. Mama Louise who mothers the whole circus. Trumpets and drums, Mrs. Baker who shines in the spotlights, animal shows, tent after tent with attractions … and an audience which has come from the end of the earth, or beyond."

Maxim put his arm around Darragh. "We're leaving tomorrow morning," he said. "Whatever may be there."

We continued talking around the campfire, in excited whispers, as if to protect our thoughts against being swallowed by the darkness. From time to time someone would walk away from the fire to see whether the light was still glowing in the distance.

Many of our neighbours talked about the circus as if they were going in search of something familiar. I didn't. "Our old existence has been snatched from under our feet, and we don't know what we got in return," I tried to explain. You nodded without conviction, and that sparked a new urge in me. I got up and bent over with a twist until my hiney was rotating in front of your face. I turned back and picked up an invisible heavy object, reeling from its imaginary weight. "But I feel like Ivan the Zot's wife, whose old rug is being replaced by" – I raised my hands as if the rug weighed nothing and let my gaze fly to the sky – "a magic carpet." One of the neighbours applauded my pantomime, and soon everyone joined in.

I felt like I could almost step on that invisible carpet and fly away. Not yet, but almost… Something irreversible in me had awakened, that's what it felt like.

I did not share the doubts and fears that kept you awake. Once the glow faded deep into the night, I flopped down on our bed, exhausted, without even undressing. You'd said you'd stay up a little longer.

I knew what I would like to do tomorrow, what I had wanted to do from the very first moment. But I didn't pressure you, Finn. Well, hardly. I'd wait until you also made that leap.

Had I slept an hour, less? You shook me awake from a dream in which I'd just mimed a door. "I finally know. I've figured it out!" You interrupted yourself and looked up, disturbed. "You'd think the neighbours could be a bit more quiet out there." You turned to me again. "Well, I'm not exactly quiet either. Pauline, I know why I have a jester's suit!

"We have been brought into this misery by that threesome, the one who knicked my watch. Beings who can do so much that they are almost omnipotent. No one has a chance to argue with them! Except… the jester is the figure who exposes the highest authority figures! Who corrects leaders, overthrows, the power behind the throne. Those bells are a sign of my authority, nothing less!"

Did I see the optimism that once made your face so irresistible, or did it more resemble greed?

You slowly felt on your back for the jester's hood and raised it up. Your hands were shaking, setting every bell on the hood jingling. The high-pitched ringing formed an overtone for the noise which came from outside.

Your hands froze when a sudden sucking pop made the door of our trailer disappear. Clammy tentacles rustled us both out. A second later, our entire trailer disappeared into the body bag of a kraken bigger than our old house. I saw tentacles fiddling with your jester suit, and then they started fondling me too. Cold mucus hit my arms, my hair, my behind… I shrieked in panic; I think you did too, but for once I was busy with myself, not with you. More and more tentacles picked us up. The last thing I saw before I lost consciousness at dawn was a mass of brick, furniture, lampposts and bicycles rushing toward us in a writhing sea of tentacles.

As I opened my eyes, I stared at our house. You and I were both lying, naked again and without the slightest trace of slime, on the lawn of our front yard. On our doormat I saw your pajamas and my jeans and T-shirt, folded the way I would have done it, and on top of your pajamas something glistened in the sun – could I trust my eyes? I looked behind me. Here and there the row of our suburban houses showed a gaping hole – that hole was where Louise and Quintin's house had stood, and the one over there….

I looked around, desperate to see where our donkey and trailer were. Nothing. Your Tesla Imperator was neatly back in its spot under the pergola. I started to cry.

You stood up. "Come on, Pauline, come in before the neighbours see us." You were energetic. I was too shocked to do anything. You took me by the shoulders and led me, trembling and spinning, into our house. In passing you quickly grabbed the watch that I'd spotted on top of your pajamas.

In the living room, filled with the furniture you'd bought, I collapsed on the llama wool rug you'd bargained for during our Andean vacation. "Where – is – our – new…." I rapped my fists against your fledgling jelly belly, "… flying…". I started crying again, hiccuping, and collapsed on the rug.

You were slumped next to the rug, arms dangling beside your body.

For half an hour you tried to hug and comfort me, but when I didn't respond, you became irritated. "Jesus, Pauline, yes, the past few days have been an ordeal, but we have our whole world back. This is not the moment to collapse, is it dear? Be happy!"

Your watch beeped, and you startled. "Shit, look at the time! I'll be getting calls from all and sundry claiming damages from the past few days. It'll be a day full of fine-print discussions."

As I lay on the rug, unable to face our old world – no, *your* old world – you changed into your smart suit. For a goodbye, you gave me a pat on my hair. "See you tonight, dear. Take care of yourself."

As you rushed out of the door, you muttered, "But I'm sure there are loads of people out there who'll want to get disaster insurance right away after this nightmare, at any cost. Maybe this won't be such a lost day after all."

The whisper of your Tesla's engine was the last I heard from you.

You may still be interested in the miraculous events I experienced after you left. And maybe not. I'll stay on the safe side: I won't waste a single word relating them. This is not a letter to explain myself, and the gods help me it is certainly not a letter to justify myself: it is merely a letter of farewell, from you and from our lives.

As a parting gift, I'll give you the only piece of advice that might be of some help to you: "Take care of yourself, dear, and pay particular attention to the fine print. It will soon become even more important."

Roelof Goudriaan has been one of the Albedo One editors since 1997.

Walking on Water
Tais Teng

Amal Khan
17 November 2168

"Come on, father!" his eldest, good for nothing, daughter called from the bobbing polystyrene float. "Please, o please, hurry. We have to be gone when the tsunami rolls in!"

Above the emergency float the balloon only slowly, almost grudgingly, filled with hydrogen. Right now it seemed a sagging blob which certainly couldn't lift his family above the monster waves rolling in from the Strait of Malacca.

After a last look at the almost empty stream bed of the Mekong and his lost orchard, Amal Khan sloshed through the ankle-deep water and climbed over the railing. The last fruit trees left were spindly growths, trying to root in the crazed, sun-baked clay. The monsoon had failed six times in a row and all Himalayan ice was gone.

The ground started to tremble and a dark line showed at the horizon. *A lion's roar*, Amal Khan thought, *the land herself voicing her agony*. Soon there would be water again, salty ocean water, and this time, with all Dutch-made dykes broken, it wouldn't go away. Bangladesh had been lying meters below sea level for the last fifty years.

"There she goes," his eldest daughter crowed and tugged at a fluorescent rope. The balloon straightened, became an inverted teardrop. Three bouncing hops and they were in the air.

The acceleration pushed his feet deep in the foam and he sat abruptly down.

Sayla was waving her hands in the air, commanding the 3D printed vessel. Suddenly he felt strangely safe. His daughter might be a spinster who at twenty-six would never get a husband and give him grandchildren, but she knew tech. She had been working for the infidel Dutch for ten years now and without their magic they would all be dead and drowned.

From three miles up the tsunami was no more than a moving line, leaving a silver sheet of permanent water in its wake. More waves would follow, Sayla's pad showed: the Tambora was still erupting, edging into supervolcanohood.

Amal Khan had always been a good Muslim, doing his ablutions and bowing to Mecca five times a day. He had never visited the holy city because where would a durian farmer find the time or the money? So he really, truly didn't understand why his god was so angry with him and his country.

"How high do we go?" his other daughter asked. "Can we see the mountains, Sayla? The Everest?"

"If we went that high we would gasp for breath and turn purple. No, just a little way, Farah. They are coming."

Amal Khan frowned. "Who? Who's coming?"

She avoided his gaze. "Meneer Wolters. Alex." She straightened and she became something alien, as far from an obedient daughter as a woman could be. "Alex Wolters. We had nowhere to go but the Netherlands still admits refugees. If they are, eh, family."

"Family!" Amal Khan quacked. "You married him!"

"Alex rather likes me so we agreed to marry. That makes me a status holder. Me and my family. Blue cards for all."

He spread his hands. "But there was no wedding, Sayla. No rice strewn. No aunts and uncles."

He really, truly didn't understand why his god was so angry with him and his country.

Some dread is too deep to really express. It meant the whole world had turned upside down. All that was familiar would be gone. He had seen Holland on the screen: towers that reached to the sky, with faces dancing among the clouds, fields of flowers that went on and on.

"I see three drones," Farah pointed. "Is that your, eh, husband?"

"Not yet, the drones will pull us to the Achmed Wilders. The dyke-laying machine."

The first drone hooked into the cables of the balloon and a voice issued from the insect-like machine: "Everything all right, love?"

"We survived. That should be enough for now."

"Yes, survive," Alex said. "But survive in style."

It was the Dutch credo, Amal knew: Survive in style. Half of the Netherlands had sunken beneath the waves that fateful November twenty years ago but the Dutch had fought back. Triple and quadruple dykes surrounded the reclaimed lands nowadays. Most of their houses could float or stood on piles.

His new son-in-law proved to be as black as a Tamil but Amal knew that the old rules of beauty no longer applied. Beautiful was what kept you safe from the sun and didn't pepper your skin with melanomas. If all went well, soon he and his daughters would turn as black. It was a pity, though: Farah had always been as white as a Bollywood princess.

"I heard about your wife," Alex said. "I am so sorry."

"She is in Paradise now. I often dream about her. She told me she is waiting for me but that there was no need to hurry."

"Good to know."

They shook hands and Amal bore down. Alex's fingers felt like solid teakwood and Amal had to give up first. *Good. Nothing wrong with being strong. This is no mouse-pusher or poem-reciter but a hands-on man. An engineer.*

There was some gray at Alex's temples, which was also right. A man shouldn't marry before he could provide for his family.

Above Amal, booms swung and he heard the roar of 3D printers which turned clay and sand into sheets of bubble concrete. "Are you building a new dyke?"

Asking a man about his work, his expertise, was always a good way to start a conversation.

"I would really like to, but there is no one left to pay us. We are heading for Taiwan. To strengthen their seawalls."

No one left to pay. Amal looked across the waves but they went on and on: even the seaside barrier of mangroves was gone. Bangladesh had become mythic, one with Atlantis and the Fiji Islands.

He heard the girls whispering behind his back. Amal had the ears of a bat: his wife had once said he could hear the worms digging beneath his feet.

"Did you?" Farah asked. "I mean, you are married now."

"Of course. The Dutch don't believe in fumble-fingered virgins. And we had a gene scan made. So our children wouldn't end up with six fingers, eh? Or without a nose."

He stepped forward some paces: there are female secrets a father is better off not knowing.

"You, we, we are going to Holland afterward?" he asked his new son-in-law.

"I sent pictures of Sayla to my parents and my sister. But they would really like to meet her face to face. You all."

Taiwan hit him hard when they debarked. So strange, so impossibly rich and organized. There had been cams in the village, of course, but those had mostly been out of order. Their lenses were filmed or cracked and didn't follow him when he crossed the street. These were alive, with tiny LEDs blinking, and no doubt some AI was noticing him. Working tech: it made Amal feel protected and cherished.

They stayed at the Shangri-La's Far Eastern Plaza Hotel in Taipei. When Amal stood on the jutting balcony the air smelt fresh, leafy. Nothing like the mudflats or the billowing dust of midsummer.

Looking down, not a single car was to be seen: e-bikes sped along roads made of tough, gene-boosted grass. Drones buzzed through the deep blue sky. He saw a whole procession of rain clouds moving in from the sea. Clearly cumulonimbus, fat with water. As a farmer, he knew his clouds and this was wealth. His own trees and bushes had been drip irrigated, each drop of water hoarded and only released when the leaves started to sag.

"Alex said it rains here almost every day."

Farah stood next to him. She wore a ring on every finger, a necklace with amber beads: no doubt presents from Alex and her big sister. "Are we going to live here?"

"Just for a month and a half. Then we'll fly to Holland."

"Fly?"

"Nothing with wings. Even Alex isn't that rich. A zeppelin."

"I see." There was a pause, an almost buzzing silence. Farah wanted to tell him something, urgently. He waited her out until she started to speak.

"She is pregnant, you know. Sayla is. She didn't want to tell you before she was further along. Didn't dare to tell you."

"I am such an ogre?" And right then he realized he had been, until quite recently. If Sayla had told him in Bangladesh, before the tsunami, he would have roared, called her a harlot. Getting pregnant before you married wasn't something a good daughter should do.

Farah looked up at his face. "You are not angry?"

I am going to be a grandfather after all! It fitted somehow. A brand new family for a brand new country. And Alex had done the right thing, married her when she became pregnant. *He must have wanted her baby.*

"How far along is she?"

"Three months. That is the safe time. If a baby goes wrong, it is before that."

He hadn't known that: such knowledge belonged to the country of women where no man was supposed to go.

"Eh, father? I think she wanted me to tell you, but I am not sure. Not really sure.'

"I'll wait till she tells me herself," he assured her.

"And act surprised?"

"That too." He involuntarily looked down at his hands and for a moment he didn't recognize them. They were no longer brown but matte black. Sunproof.

The zeppelin rose to the stratosphere, where the new hothouse winds were blowing, fierce as demons. Solar cells drank the searing sunlight and powered a hundred rotors.

In the evening India appeared on the horizon and during the next days, they crossed the Afghan badlands, the Khanates of Novaya Rossiya.

It was like being an ant, it seemed to Amal, crawling across an immense, ever-changing map. The sunsets were invariably gorgeous: the super-volcano had filled the whole atmosphere with dust and sulfur aerosols.

Sayla's belly wasn't exactly bulging but it was unmistakable now he knew. Amal hadn't asked yet if it was a son or a daughter. No doubt Sayla knew: the Dutch could look right into your body and see the heart of an unborn beating in glorious full-color. His daughter had never shunned knowledge.

When they had passed the Caspian Sea Sayla knocked on his door.

"Farah told you," Sayla stated. It sounded like an accusation.

He nodded. "And I replied that any grandchild of mine is more than welcome."

He saw her smile bloom like an opening orchid and could well understand why Alex thought her beautiful. *I just have never given her a good reason to smile.*

"It will be a son," his daughter said. "We'll call him Thomas Amal. To honor both our fathers."

"Thank you."

"If it had been a daughter her name would be Alexa Nishad." The name of his dead wife. He felt tears sting in the corners of his eyes.

"Home," Alex declared and Amal heard the pride in his voice.

They stood in front of the huge diamond window in the bow. Holland from on high was spider-webbed with channels, silver threads in the green. Dykes formed concentric circles, spreading from the higher ground.

It looks like a beleaguered fortress, Amal thought, *ready for any assault the sea can muster for the next century.* Perhaps it would even stop the kind of tsunami that drowned his own country?

Alex pointed and the interactive window drew a circle. "That is where we'll live. Egmond-at-Sea, right at the top of the tallest dyke." The window zoomed in on a white villa with a dozen balconies and bay windows. A twenty-meter high windmill stood in front, her vanes ponderously turning.

"You must be wealthy!" Amal heard himself exclaim. A faux pas and he tried

It was the Dutch credo, Amal knew: Survive in style.

to recover with: "Or do all the Dutch live that well?"

"It isn't mine. Only my official residence. Taiwan was my last tour. I'm the *dijkgraaf* of Noord-Holland now."

The window instantly drew an oval which included a hundred miles of dykes and canals. Amal understood that Sayla had married up, right into the aristocracy. *Alex must be some kind of rajah, an honored protector against the sea.*

"Can I have my own room?" Farah asked and somehow that made it real. *I am here. My daughters will lack for nothing.*

How did that saying of his favorite poet go? *All the comforts of home and then some?*

According to Alex, the next city boasted a huge mosque. While he pedaled to Alkmaar on his e-bike, Amal saw the minarets rising above the hydroponic farms, topped by blue and green flames. The fields were covered with frost which glittered in the rising sun. It was the first real winter in a hundred years, Alex had told him, and it wouldn't last. A volcano winter, he had called it, because of all the ash in the sky.

The voice of the muezzin greeted him when he took off his shoes. "La illah illa Allah…"

Amal was the only bearded worshiper. No matter: a beard was no real badge of devotion and he would ask Alex if he should shave it off. He didn't want to be the rustic, set-in-his-ways father for his daughters.

Almost everybody wore a jet-black skin in this new country: that at least wouldn't set them apart as strangers. It was also nice not to have to calculate who was the better or the lesser, gauging the darkness of any skin you encountered.

He located the *qiblah*, the niche in the wall which indicated Mecca, and tried to empty his head, reciting the name of Allah and his prophet.

After some time others walked into the hall until they formed long rows. All bowed down and the imam intoned the *salaat*, the common prayer. The words were like a warm bath and he felt the U*mmah* surrounding him, that great brotherhood of all believers.

I am but a drop in the ocean of the Ummah, he thought, *and the Merciful sees us all, knows the footfall of the tiniest mouse.*

When he stepped on his e-bike a sudden jab in his side made him hiss in pain. He took a deep breath but the pain grew, multiplied until it became a white-hot throbbing.

I am but a drop in the ocean of the Ummah, and the Merciful sees us all, knows the footfall of the tiniest mouse.

"Shall I call your daughter?" his antique Huawei asked. "You seem to be in some distress."

"Please. Yes, please."

"Calling."

The pain jumped into his head and all thought stopped in a white-out.

He woke under a blue sky with swallows darting under the far clouds. No doubt a projection.

The pain had gone but when he tried to lift his arm nothing happened. It remained at his side, inert as the limb of a showroom dummy.

"Where am I?" he said, *tried* to say, but it came out a grunt.

A face appeared in his field of vision. A physician probably: he was wearing smart-glasses that could probably look right into his brain.

"What? What is wrong with me?"

"Cancer. Metastasized through your entire body. Impossible to operate."

It probably was no real physician, but a mock-man, an android. Even the greatest quack would have better bedside manners.

"There must be something you can do!" he heard Sayla cry. "This is Holland! You can do *anything*."

The android rubbed his chin but that only pulled him deeper into the uncanny valley. "I can probably cut out his brain. Save it." He touched Amal's brow. "No. Just too far gone."

"And virtual?" Alex asked. "Make a brain-scan and load that in an artificial body?"

Amal discovered he could ball his fists.

"I don't want to become a robot! Just let me die. I am *ready* to die. Nishad is waiting for me. My wife, she is in Paradise."

But then something happened which every true believer dreaded. He lost his certainty. All his life he had felt the presence of the Merciful when he needed Him most, somebody all-wise and powerful standing just behind his shoulder, smiling down on him.

He suddenly knew this was it: one life and nothing after it. A hideous void from before he was born and ever afterward. No Paradise and not even a Hell. Worst of all nobody was waiting for him.

"Save me," he whispered. "Anything. Any way."

"As you wish."

Thomas
6 June 2176

Thomas-Amal's father was the strongest man on the whole dyke, his mother the most beautiful woman he knew and one day he would marry her. His aunt Farah lived in the house, too, and she brought a new boyfriend home every week. She seldom had time to play with him.

His grandfather always had, though. Amal sometimes wore a false-flesh body or the grass mower, but he mostly sat in a little box with arms and clever legs.

His other two grandparents lived far, far away, monitoring the rapidly melting glaciers of Antarctica. He only saw them on birthdays.

That summer day he was walking the dyke with his father. The Outer-dyke was forty meters tall and quite smart, flexing with every incoming wave. The sea might only have risen two meters but hurricanes made for truly high waves which hit like watery avalanches.

"I want to be a *dijkgraaf*, too," Thomas declared. With his father, he was always *Thomas*, while his grandfather invariably called him *Amal*.

"That is quite possible. But you'll have to study a lot."

"I can do that. I am clever. My phone says I am in the IQ 140 range."

"Right. That is understood then. You'll become the next *dijkgraaf*."

Alex's phone rang and Thomas saw his father stiffen. Alex was a very busy man, but the Sunday walks on the dyke with his son were sacred, of the only-a call-me-in-a-dire-emergency kind.

"Sorry, Thomas. I have to take this."

Thomas had never seen his father afraid.

"You are sure, Alexa? Of course, you are sure. I'll call the other *dijkgraven*. Put the system on code red. Hitch the dikes up to the highest level. Close the flood barriers."

"Something wrong?" Thomas asked.

"That was your grandmother. The Antarctic Ring of Fire went off. There are a hundred and twenty volcanoes sitting under the ice. And they all blew. Like a string of goddamn firecrackers."

Every Dutch boy knows about the sea level. "How much more?"

"Three meters. But the ice won't melt all at once. We may have some time. Years."

He kept talking to his phone and a quarter of an hour later the dyke started to rumble. Sheets of black diamond went up, five meters, ten, and then locked together. At the same time, the windmills stilled and retracted their vanes.

"Will there be a storm?" he asked his father.

"Perhaps. The whole weather system is going haywire." He raised the phone. "Alexa? Mother, you are still there?" He shook his head. "Only a hiss. Shit!"

Thomas never saw his grandparents again. Half of the Ross ice shelf had slipped into the sea and the monster waves had swamped their research vessel.

The Antarctic wasn't exactly close. It took a week before the sky turned black. A force eleven storm blew the top of the waves into spume, strewed salty hail across the land. But the dykes held.

Most of them, and Zeeland had been inundated before. The inhabitants had the same mentality as the farmers in Tornado Alley. Come up from the storm cellars when the howling stopped and start to rebuild. In this case, that meant putting on an aqualung and inflating a rubber boat. The dykes knew how to repair themselves and had thousands of pumps built-in.

Thomas
24 February 2192

The *Engineer Lely Instituut voor Hoger Watermanagement* was drifting just above the Doggersbank, one of those sunken lands where Neanderthals once had hunted mammoths and giant deer. Build on pontoons of black diamond it was weatherproof up to a force twelve hurricane and could survive anything short of a category three monster wave.

Thomas fitted right in: these were all workaholic girls and boys who loved to learn and looked down on power games and one-upmanship as a perfect waste of time. They only asked that no one hindered them while they did as good a job as possible.

In his second year, he took the course which was curiously titled The Psychology of Water. Now water and all her interactions formed a huge field, with no less than nine phase changes, but he had never heard of water as thinking or forming slow nervous networks like the toadstools or forests.

Engineers like hands-on and seeing is believing: the course started with a glass bowl filled with milky seawater and an electron microscope.

He sat down next to the red-haired girl with eyes as green as polished tourmaline and a clever fox face. Probably a refugee from the Irish Troubles. Thomas sneaked a look at her social profile: Agatha Collins. I love turtles and hurricane surfing!!!

"I took this sample from the sea just this morning," their instructor said. "Disregard the plankton and the silt; zoom in on the microplastics."

The ocean was saturated with beads of plastic, Thomas knew, anything from sand-sized grains to submicroscopic. Three years before the *dijkgraven* had seeded the North Sea with nanos whose only programming was: locate every piece of microplastic and carry them to the collection point.

"There you are. Do you see the nanos swarming around every little piece?"

The nanos looked alive, like amoebas, with extremely long cilia. They trailed like the tentacles of a jellyfish and the water around them looked thick somehow.

"Their cilia are hydrophilic," the instructor said. "Each nanomachine rules a bubble of water at least half a centimeter across." He brought his phone to his lips, spoke a code word.

The water started to move, swirled around in a whirlpool which soon encompassed the whole bowl. A new word and the whirlpool switched direction.

"They obey you?" the girl, Agatha, asked.

"Not exactly. Only when they are in the mood. They are self-organizing. A swarm. And evolving fast."

"And they are everywhere," Agatha said. "Doing what they want."

"That is why the course is called The psychology of Water. We have to understand them. Learn to talk with them with more than simple commands."

That evening Thomas walked the panzer-glass boulevard around the institute with Agatha. The sunset made a gorgeous bonfire encompassing half the sky.

When he kissed her lips they tasted salty.

Amal
9 November 2196

He went in a false-flesh body to the graduation of his grandson, holding the hands of his two granddaughters. Some people frowned on incarnated souls, calling them *tick-tocks* or *little better than robots*.

"Is our Thomas a *dijkgraaf* now?" little Hyacinth asked.

"That will take some time. He is just starting out. A hydraulic engineer. That is still a long way from *dijkgraaf*."

"He'll be the best *dijkgraaf* ever," Amelie piped up. "Build us a dyke as tall as the sky. So tall not even a seagull can fly over it."

The ceremony was beautiful in its own way. Thomas-Amal emerged clad in a mantle of seagrass from the waiting room and he wore an ancient diving mask that had been in the family for simply ages. The director handed him the diploma which was written with squid ink on a sheet of pressed seaweed.

"Survive," she said and the hall responded with a heartfelt "But survive in style."

Thomas's girlfriend embraced him and then the handshaking started.

"Come," Amal said. "The rest will be so boring. Let's score some cupcakes before all the pink ones are gone."

Amelia giggled. "You can't even eat."

"But I can taste. Even if I have to spit the crumbs out afterward."

Thomas

"Save me," he whispered. "Anything. Any way."

"We have to talk," his father said. "Before you get drunk with your friends."

"No problem."

"Well, we have one." He folded his arms. "I need you. We need you. We can make you an aspirant *dijkgraaf*. Jump you four command levels up.'

Thomas frowned. "Won't they call that nepotism?"

"They will, but you are our best

water-psychologist. It is a field so new no *dijkgraaf* really understands it."

"What is there to understand? We seeded nanos in the oceans to gather all the microplastics and bring them to the shore. Part of the plastic they use to construct more nanomachines."

"You told me once they swarm. That they are getting intelligent."

"Intelligent is a great word. Not even as clever as a cat."

Which was a barefaced lie. The *dijkgraven* would never accept that the nanomachines now controlled the sea currents. They had already reversed the Arctic Waterfall, the cold water that streamed from Greenland's melting glaciers and had halted the Gulf Stream a generation ago. It was one of great recent enigmas and only Thomas and his colleagues had seen the link with the nanos. It was their problem now.

"Not even as clever as a cat?" His father looked at him in that special half searching, half sardonic way. "You never could tell a lie well. We need them. Making the dykes higher is no longer an option. The water is still rising. Rising faster than we can build and that last half meter was half a meter too much. The glaciers of Greenland are still moving. We have to stop the new water before it reaches the North Sea." He reached in the air and a map appeared.

A dyke stretched from Free Scotland to Norway. In the South, a second dam closed off the Channel. The North Sea Enclosure, the title proclaimed.

Thomas got a sinking feeling in the pit of his stomach. The *dijkgraven* had reached the limits of their inventiveness and had fled into fantasy.

"A beautiful dream, but impractical. I would take us a century to construct something this gigantic. To keep the Atlantic Ocean out. Gigatonnes of sand, teratonnes. There isn't enough sand in the whole North Sea to print…'

"You're right of course. And we don't have a century." A flick of his wrist and diagrams marched in front of them, moving lines that jumped into the red time after time.

"So short!"

"Five years. At most. Then the dykes will start to buckle. System overload. Critical water mass."

Thomas looked back at the map, zoomed in. The projected dykes would have to be at least half a kilometer wide and sixty meters high. More material than all the dykes of the world combined.

"We need the nanos," his father said. "They can build us a dyke of living water. Talk to them. We know you can."

A video appeared. Thomas stood with his feet in a tide pool at the bottom of the Outer-dyke. A column of water was rising. It stretched a tentacle of whirling water and encircled Thomas' wrist.

"You are water, too," the creature said. "Water that walks on the land. How curious." The voice was high and pure as a glass flute. "Come walk with me."

"Walk with you?" But Thomas didn't hesitate and stepped on the surface. It felt like rubber, he remembered, flexing rubber and curiously stiff, as if surfaced with a non-slip coating.

"Talk to them," his father said. "Promise them anything they want."

"There is no them," Thomas said. "Just one being. Huge as the ocean. As all the seven Seas."

He had only tried it once before, descending the dyke and emitting their come-hither-code with his phone. There had been a full moon, too. He went down the stairs and the sea seemed to breathe, an enormous beast. Which wasn't a metaphor at all.

A stir in the corner of his eye. A small box was descending the stairs, the twin camera eyes glowing.

"Amal?" he said. "Grandfather, what are you doing here?"

"I want to watch you walking on the water. I always fancied having a holy man in the family."

"Right. Just don't laugh when I only end up with a wet coat and sodden shoes."

Thomas was sure the sea had heard his call, though. An oily sheen was spreading across the waves, an unnatural stiffness creeping into every breaker. He took a step and the water held.

One of the waves stopped in mid curl and formed an enormous face.

"It is an interesting idea," the creature said. "Building a dyke to stop myself. We can reverse the flow too. Pump the water away and lay the ancient Doggerlands bare."

"You'll do it?"

"For a price. We want to walk the drylands like you. Unhindered."

"Great. We have an agreement."

"We need one more thing. A template to build our bodies. You."

"You want to take me apart? Kill me?"

"We have to see it all. Every cell and bone. Putting everything back afterward seems impractical. Like reconstructing scrambled eggs and putting them back in the shell."

Thomas was the son of a *dijkgraaf*. "If that is what is needed."

"No, wait!" Amal cried. "Take me. I am older. Much more interesting than a young man."

"You are only silicon and plastic. Just like us. No water. Your request is denied."

The sea rose to Thomas' knees and Amal saw him dissolve, a man-shaped piece of sugar.

I should have known, he thought. *Gods always ask for a human sacrifice.*

The moment Thomas was no more than a red stain, a wall of water rose, curling away from the land.

It ascended, soon higher than the dyke, then even overtopping the windmills. A moment of perfect stasis followed while Amal waited for it to crash down, to break the puny dyke.

But no, it started to move, rolled to the moonlit horizon. A second wave rose and sped to the East to block the Channel.

Tais Teng has published several stories in Albedo One.

The End of the Road

Juliet E. McKenna

'Is this it?' Sayesta sounded mildly curious.

Toko and Lesh weren't fooled. This past half-year, they'd seen plenty of people relax, thinking they were safe when they heard that casual tone from the swordswoman. That was generally an instant before the poor fools learned how very wrong they could be. The boys exchanged a glance. They could do that safely since they were riding ten paces or more behind her, looking after the pack mules.

'Well, there's no more map left, so it must be.' Riding beside Sayesta, Evrine waved the grimy sheaf of paper in her many-ringed hand.

Toko and Lesh had seen that long, long, painstakingly inked strip unfolded, studied, marked up and refolded so often that it was a wonder the winding route could still be read. The map was barely in one piece, splitting along so many of its creases. The brothers exchanged another grimace.

'There's no need for you two to look like that.' Evrine turned in her saddle to grin at them. 'Exciting, isn't it?'

'Yes, mistress,' Toko assured her.

Lesh nodded vigorously. When they had some privacy, fetching water or fodder for the mules or grooming the horses, he and Toko debated long and hard whether Evrine was a mage as well as the scholar she undoubtedly was. Lesh argued she must be a mage. She seemed to know what they were thinking or doing so often. Surely there was no way that she could have any idea without using magic to read their minds. Toko had pointed out how often Mam had known exactly what they were up to, when nobody could have told her, and they knew for a certainty that Mam was no mage.

Lesh looked at the map Evrine was stuffing into the pocket of her cloak. She had promised they could have it when she was done with this journey. He and Toko would need the map to get home, checking off the villages, bridges, crossroads, notable trees and hills that would confirm they were on the right road, More than once on their way here, the lack of such faithfully recorded landmarks had proved they were on the wrong road. They'd been forced to retrace their steps to the last place they were sure of and try again. The journey back would surely be easier, going in the other direction.

Now there was no more road. They had arrived, barely halfway through the mild afternoon, with the branches on the trees greening with the first touch of spring and a few clusters of blossom in the thickets perfuming the breeze.

But what was this place? They were looking at a solid, wide stone building with three rows of windows below its shallow tiled roof and stubby chimneys. In the centre, three stone steps led up to a double door. It looked as if it belonged in a prosperous town's main square. It reminded Lesh of the halls where landowners and merchants met to agree the season's prices for wool or wheat or wine or whatever else their particular district produced in enough surplus to sell. Evrine had explained how such deals were done, that first time Lesh and Toko had gaped in astonishment at the imposing surroundings when they had first arrived in a prosperous town.

He looked at the topmost windows and wondered if there were bedrooms up there. That had been another revelation on this journey. Rooms with separate beds raised up off the floor, and sometimes even rooms with just one bed for only one person. No house they had ever set foot in before had more than a sleeping loft crammed with straw-stuffed mattresses, above the long room where everybody lived, and reached by a ladder.

No one in their village was interested in building upwards. Luxury was a house wide enough for everyone to get close to the hearth in winter, and long enough to get away from the cooking fire in summer. No one was fool enough to have big windows squandering precious heat in the bitter cold, or letting in the scorching harvest sun.

This building was no merchants' exchange though. It stood alone in this hollow below the rising swell of a tree-covered hill. The last hamlet worth the name was eight days ride behind them, and no one there had ever heard tell of anyone living out this way.

Lesh had been about to ask the matron who brewed the hamlet's ale, where did she think the road went then? Who would go to the trouble of clearing this broad path and laying down cartloads of gravel, however long ago that had been done? But Evrine had caught his eye and she had shaken her head, not much, but just enough to make Lesh bite his tongue. Toko could say what he liked. Lesh still thought Evrine was a mage.

'So how do we get inside to find this treasure of yours?' Sayesta studied the windows and the entrance with keen interest. She was always alert and energetic, no matter how long the day's ride might have been. No matter how old she might be. That was something else the brothers had debated without coming to any conclusions. The swordswoman's short-cropped hair was more white than grey, and her face was deeply lined. That reminded them both of Gammer, who only moved from her chair by the fire for meals at the long table, to visit the privy, or to go to her bed behind the screen Da had made when she couldn't climb the ladder to the loft any more. But Sayesta could climb a tall tree or scale a wall around a yard as easily as Toko. They had seen her do both and more besides on this journey.

Lesh looked at Toko again. Every window they could see was tightly shuttered and the iron-studded door at the top of those three broad steps looked equally secure.

Evrine wasn't concerned. 'Let's look around the back.'

Nothing bothered Evrine. At least nothing had so far on this journey. Well, not while Lesh and Toko had been travelling with the two women. They had no idea how long the women had been on the road before they had taken a wrong turn and arrived at the village way out in the wheat lands that was all the world Lesh and Toko had ever known.

All they had known until Da had agreed to let them go on this journey, when he had finished putting new shoes on the four horses and two mules that the women had been trying to manage between them, ever since their previous grooms had got bored and run away. At least, that's what Evrine had said, while they were waiting for Ma's medicine to work on the light-coated mule which had eaten something it shouldn't.

Talking it over later, Toko and Lesh had decided those slackwits, whoever they might have been, had run off because they were scared of Sayesta. To be fair, they had soon learned she could be terrifying without even raising her voice.

The swordswoman looked around at the boys and grinned. 'Come on, you two.'

Toko looked at Lesh. They shared a shrug. As Evrine and Sayesta nudged their horses into a walk, the boys did the same, tugging on the leading reins to get the mules moving.

As they went around to the back, the building turned out to make three sides of a hollow square surrounding a paved yard. Thick drifts of wind-blown dead leaves were piled high in the corners. Those must be from last autumn and any number of autumns before that, judging by the dark stains on the paving. There were three doors; one in the centre of each wing on both sides, and another one straight ahead which must be opposite that main entrance where the road arrived.

Another building ran across the fourth side of the paved square, separated from the main whatever-it-was by a broad path. Half of it had two rows of windows as securely shuttered as the rest, and a solid oak door. The other half was as welcome as it was familiar.

'Stables,' Toko said, relieved.

He didn't have to be a mage to know that. Those doors and that hatch for the hayloft were unmistakable, even if the walls were masonry as finely crafted as the main – house? Who would want to live all the way out here? What did they eat? They were several days ride beyond the last tilled fields and pastures. Lesh shook his head, bemused.

Sayesta snapped her fingers to get his attention. She jerked her head at the stables. 'You two see what's in there while we look for a way to find the treasure.'

She dismounted with her usual ease. She never seemed to get stiff in the saddle. Evrine took her time, more or less sliding off her horse. Her boots hit the ground with a thud that ruffled her layers of skirts and petticoats. Where Sayesta was lithe and lean, Evrine was comfortably plump with long braids framing her cheerful round face. Her hair was as blue as a harvest season sky, and that was something else that made Lesh think she must be a mage. As to whether she was older or younger than Sayesta, he couldn't possibly guess.

He dismounted and gathered up the women's reins to lead their horses to the stable, as well as his own mount and the dark-coated mule. Toko had already got the doors open without any difficulty.

'This place wasn't locked?' Lesh was surprised, as he led the animals inside. One of the first things he'd learned on this journey was how much folk who lived along the road feared people they didn't know getting into their homes and stealing their things. No one bothered with locks at home. There wasn't much of anything to steal, and anyone who tried would soon be found out, since everyone knew everyone else.

'No, just bolted top and bottom.' Toko had already led his horse and the light-coated mule into the dimness. 'Open that door at the end, will you?'

Lesh left the animals to their own devices and did as Toko asked. Throwing open this second door shed more light on the spacious, clean-swept stalls along the back wall. There were hooks for harness opposite, above rests for saddles, and benches for sitting and working, as well as bins that had surely once held grain. The mules and the horses made satisfied noises as they recognised such surroundings.

Toko sniffed like a hound searching for a trail. 'No one's had horses in here for a dog's age.'

Lesh agreed. All he could smell was dry stone and dust. He opened one of the grain bins. 'There's nothing in here. No sign of rats though.'

Hopefully it would be a good long while before it occurred to any local vermin that things hereabouts might have changed. If rats did turn up, they would have to find a cat. If they were going to be staying here long enough for that to matter.

Lesh swallowed a lump in his throat. He still missed the cats back home. More than he missed his little brothers and sisters, truth be told. He reminded himself what Da had said, back when the fields had bristled with stubble and the thickets were turning gold. Him and Toko, they were doing their duty by the little ones, going on this journey. Mam and Da would have two less mouths to feed through the coldest months, and when they came home, they'd bring two horses back with them as well as a purse of silver. Along with the coin Sayesta had already given Da, everyone would feel the benefit for the rest of the year and likely longer.

Neither Toko nor Lesh had argued. This had to be better way to spend the winter than labouring on local farms when extra hands were needed for some freezing and filthy task. The cold meant calls on the blacksmith's time and skills came fewer and further between, so Da seldom had need of them in the forge.

Sudden clanking startled him out of those recollections. At the other end of the building, Toko had found a pump. He was working the handle up and down. As water gushed from the spout to fill the basin, he cheered. 'Well, we don't need to go hunting for a stream.'

'They'll still need some fodder, and some sort of bedding, if we can find it.' Lesh grabbed the dark-coated mule's halter as she headed for the pump. She knew her own mind and was often inclined to try getting her own way.

This time, she decided to follow Lesh to the closest stall. He and Toko tied up the patient beasts and stripped off their harness and saddles. Toko found an iron-bound bucket and used it to fill the stone water troughs from the pump. By the time he had finished, the dried-out wooden staves had swelled enough to stop the bucket leaking, more or less.

While he was doing that, Lesh went outside, around to the back of the stables. He found a broad stretch of tussocky grass running away up the long slope to the trees. There was enough fresh green to give the horses and mules a treat, as well as yellowed growth to cut and heap in the stalls in place of wheat straw. If he could find a scythe. He remembered there were tools on pegs on the wall by the pump.

Toko was way ahead of him, as was so often the case. Sitting on the stone mounting block by the stable door, he looked up as Lesh rounded the corner of the building. He'd found a scythe and a sickle, and he was putting a fresh edge on their blades with his whetstone.

'Can you believe no one's been in here to help themselves to good tools like these?'

'Maybe they had good reason to stay away.' Lesh looked at the other building. 'So they never discussed coming here. So no one who came after them even knew where this place was to be found.'

'Until Evrine found her map.' Toko handed Lesh the sickle. 'Right, let's get to work.'

Toko was like that, like Da, always focused on what needed doing next. Maybe that was because he was the eldest, even if there wasn't even a full year between them. Lesh tried to do the same, but he couldn't help his mind wandering as he worked. Where had Evrine found that map? How far had she and Sayesta travelled? He wondered what the map would show him, if he unfolded whatever was left, after they had followed the route back home.

None of this stopped him doing his fair share of the work. He'd learned long ago how to let his mind roam free while his muscles were toiling. Soon he and Toko were gathering up armfuls of fodder for the horses and mules. As they came back around to the stables, they found Sayesta by the open door to the other half of the stable building.

'How did you open that?' Lesh really hoped she would say she had used magic, now they had reached their journey's end.

The swordswoman grinned and held up a handful of what looked like keys that had been through a famine. 'Lock picks.'

Toko was already peering through the door into the gloom. 'It's a kitchen. Huge.'

'Open the shutters and let in some air,' Sayesta ordered. 'See what you can find by way of firewood, and let me know what provisions we have left.'

'Right.' Toko went through the door, looking around with interest.

Lesh was still staring at the other building. 'Why isn't the kitchen in there?'

Sayesta chuckled. 'Go and see. Go on.' She gestured at the closest door when he hesitated. 'That's open.'

He didn't need telling a third time. 'I'll be quick,' he called out to Toko.

He hurried over, but when he got to the door, he hesitated. His stomach was as hollow as that dried-out, empty old bucket. Lesh clenched his fists to stop his hands shaking. He was a grown man, as good as anyway. Next year would be his fourteenth summer so he'd have a voice in village meetings, when he and Toko got home. His nostrils flared as he drew a deep, determined breath.

He went in and saw that Evrine had opened the windows on the far wall in order to unfasten the shutters. Dust motes stirred by the breeze sparkled in the shafts of sunlight. Lesh looked around, open-mouthed. Every bit of wall that wasn't windows was shelves filled with books. All sorts of books, from weighty volumes that would need two strong hands to lift, to small, squat ones like the handful that Evrine kept in her saddlebag.

Those weren't the same books she'd had with her, when him and Toko had started travelling with the women. Lesh had seen Evrine trading the ones she had read for something new whenever she got the chance. She haggled ruthlessly with the balding, bearded men who answered her summons to whatever inn they were staying in. Mam would have admired her skills.

Lesh wondered who could possibly have bargained and bartered for all these books. This room ended in an archway cutting through a wall covered with still more shelves, and he could see another room just the same as this one. How long had it taken to fill this huge building? For whatever reason, he had no doubt all the rooms and shelves were full. He sniffed the dusty air. There was no hint of damp or rot. Had master builders made sure these walls and this roof were proof against years of storms? Or was there some magic at work?

'Isn't this marvellous?' Evrine was beaming with delight.

She stood by one of the long, leather-topped tables that ran down the centre of the room, flanked by high-backed chairs. Every table had books neatly stacked at either end. Evrine caressed the shiny-edged pages of the one lying open in front of her.

So this was the treasure she and Sayesta had been seeking. Lesh knew better than to protest there was no silver to be seen. He would have done just that, of course, when they set out on this journey. He'd learned a lot since then. Sayesta had told him and Toko that knowledge had a value beyond mere coin.

They'd already known that, of course. Da's word was respected and his opinions carried weight because he knew the secrets of working metals. He could see the exact colour that told him to strike as iron cooled from white-hot to red. He could hear the quality of brass in the note that rang out when the metal was struck. Ma knew more about dosing beasts and people than anyone within five days' walk. The smell of leaves rubbed between her fingertips told her when to gather herbs at their most potent. The precise shade of a tincture or an infusion showed her when it was ready for use. No one ever refused Mam a favour.

But Lesh hadn't realised that knowledge could be written down and traded. Now he knew that, he could see this really was a treasure house. No wonder whoever had built it hadn't wanted to risk a kitchen fire spreading through these rooms. He walked over to the closest table and opened the closest book to a random page.

'Oh.' He couldn't hide his surprise.

Evrine looked up. 'What is it?'

'I can't read this. I mean, I can, but I can't.' Lesh recognised the letters neatly written – no, he realised, neatly printed – on the page. Evrine had taught him and Toko both to read, when bad weather had kept them in an inn for five days, when she realised that neither of them knew more than their own names. But the words in this book made no sense to him.

Evrine came around the table to see what he was looking at. 'Ah.' She nodded as if she had solved a mystery. 'That's Taspian.'

Lesh looked at her for an explanation. Evrine liked explaining things.

'Taspia is to the north and west of Astamy. It's a mountainous realm beyond a mighty river, where the Astamini never gained a foothold. To this day, the Taspians keep to their own language when they write things down, even though they use Astamy script.'

Lesh nodded. Even out in the wheat lands, most folk learned a few words of Astamy alongside their mother tongue, in case they had dealings with travellers along the road when they took their harvest to market. When he and Toko got back home, they'd be the most fluent trade speakers in the whole district. He'd never heard of Taspia though.

Evrine flipped back the pages to see the front of the book. 'Oh,' she said with interest. 'This is a study of the marsh flowers and trees in Elbry.'

Lesh had never heard of Elbry either. Come to that, he hadn't known he had been born in a realm called Hukell, until Evrine had told him and Toko the river they were crossing marked the border between Hukell and Pritin.

He realised Evrine was already reading the first page of the Taspian writing. Once she got deep into a book, she could ignore a tavernful of folk complete with a performing troubadour or a spreading fist-fight. He spoke loudly to make sure she heard him.

'What do I do now, Mistress?'

'What?' As Evrine looked up from the book, her eyes were distant. She focused on Lesh and smiled. 'Whatever Sayesta tells you.'

He ducked his head obediently and went back out into the yard. Sayseta was nowhere to be seen so he headed for the kitchen. Toko had got the shutters open and checked that the pump in there worked too. Lesh marvelled at the notion of having a pump – having more than one pump – inside a building instead of in the village square for everyone to use.

Tesh was using a wet rag to wipe the dust off the table. That was salt-scrubbed wood, just like at home, with plain stools set around it. The pots and pans on the shelves, the cooking tools hung on the walls, and the fireplace with its iron hooks and roasting spit were equally reassuringly familiar. Doors around the walls promised store cupboards.

Toko looked up as Lesh came through the door.

'Let's bring the food in here.'

'Right.'

Stacking everything on the table didn't take long. The bread and fresh greens they'd bought in the hamlet were long gone, but they still had plenty of cheese, some lard, leathery dried venison, slices of dried apple and plums, the hard travel bread that Sayesta called biscuit, a fair supply of flour and the sack of dried pease that Evrine replenished at every opportunity. They wouldn't go hungry, not for a while at least. Sayesta's little chest of fragrant herbs would give them something more interesting to drink than water.

Toko started searching the shelves for some particular size of pot. 'Get some firewood, will you?'

'Right.' Lesh went outside and headed for the woods at the top of the slope behind the building. There hadn't been much rain for the past few days, so the odds were good he'd find dead wood that was dry enough to burn. He studied the grass for signs of rabbit paths or hares' nests. If they were going to be here for more than a few days, he would set some snares. They would need to save enough food to get them back to the hamlet without tightening their belts too far.

He reached the edge of the woodland and started looking through the leaf litter and tangles of last year's undergrowth. Gathering an armful of suitable sticks, he dumped them in the shelter of a jagged stump where a storm had snapped the crown off a mighty tree. That would give them more than enough fuel for the kitchen, if he and Toko could find the tools to hack off the branches and split the dead length of trunk. For now though, he'd settle for easier rewards.

As he went deeper into the woods gathering more sticks, he heard something strange. It sounded like a storm thrashing through a forest's branches, but there was barely a breath of wind. Looking up, he saw something else strange ahead. Sunlight was streaming through the trees at the top of the hill. He could see the sky. This wasn't the start of a forest at all.

So what was on the other side, if this was as far as the road went? Lesh dropped his sticks and struggled up the increasingly steep slope. When he got to the top, he was glad he was out of breath. If he hadn't been, he might have been running. If he'd done that, where would he be now, as Da so often said.

He'd be down on those rocks, smashed to a bloody pulp. Lesh dropped to his hands and knees and edged forward to the broken edge of the turf. The land was as ragged as piecrust or a torn loaf of bread, hanging over a drop of half a furrow length, maybe more. Down below, he saw water frothing white around the jagged rocks, and darker green where the pools were calmer. That was what was making the noise.

Lesh had never seen so much water. He sat back on his heels and gazed at the vast expanse shading from green to blue until it finally met the sky at some unimaginably distant horizon.

Sayesta dropped to the ground beside him. 'I'm guessing you've never seen the ocean.'

Lesh had never even heard that word.

He managed to find his voice. 'I guess that explains why the road stops here.'

Sayesta laughed as if he'd made some splendid joke. 'True enough.'

Lesh stared at the water some more. Sayesta sat beside him in companionable silence. Eventually he forced himself to look away from the – the ocean. Inside his head, he heard the sound the water made on the rocks woven into the word.

'So what are you going to do here, you and Evrine?' Him and Toko, they hadn't had the nerve to ask where they were going before, but what harm could curiosity do now?

'We're staying,' Sayesta said easily. 'It's time we settled in one place to write the last verse of our ballad.'

'On your own?' Startled, Lesh spoke without thinking. 'How will you manage?'

Sayesta laughed. 'We won't be on our own for long. We'll give you two plenty of letters to pass on when you head back along the road. A whole host of scholars will seek permission to come and see what Evrine's found. I plan to make it known that I'm setting up a sword school, in case anyone thinks they can turn up and help themselves to the books.'

She sounded as confident as always. Lesh wondered what she would do if a whole gang of marauders turned up to loot and burn this place before her allies arrived. He'd heard tell of such raiders storming up and down the road, ever since he was old enough to ask Da why he was making swords and spearheads for the boys who would be acknowledged as men of the village at midsummer. Did Sayesta think she could hold off such fearsome thieves on her own?

Her thoughts were elsewhere. 'I'll be interested to see what sword manuals and military treatises are on those shelves. There's no telling what we might find.'

Lesh had no idea what a treatise might be, and he didn't bother asking. The fascinating view of the water had drawn his eyes again.

'Will there be books about the – the ocean?' He pronounced the unfamiliar word with care.

'Of course.' Sayesta didn't doubt it. 'And travellers' tales about the lands beyond, I'll wager.'

'Beyond?' Lesh choked on his disbelief. 'There's – ?'

'You didn't think this shore was the end of the world, did you?' Sayesta was surprised, but she wasn't mocking Lesh. She never did, any more than Evrine made him or Toko feel small when something the brothers didn't know came up in conversation. 'No, there are strings of islands out there, and another great land beyond them. People along this coast build boats – they call them ships – big enough to carry folk with their beasts and supplies from one shore to another.'

Lesh stared at the vast expanse of water with its complete absence of landmarks and wondered how anyone could ever find their way across it.

Sayesta got to her feet. 'Come on, lad. Toko will be wanting his firewood.'

Lesh followed the swordswoman down the slope, away from the ocean. They picked up sticks as they walked through the trees. When they got back to the kitchen, they found Toko had gathered enough wood to get a small fire started in the hearth. A griddle was warming on the hook above it, and a pot of pease was soaking for tomorrow to one side. Lesh took the sticks and fed the fire until it was blazing. He stacked the rest in the chimney corner. Sayesta pulled out a stool and sat down at the table.

'There's rooms with beds and chairs above here. No mattresses though, or blankets.' Toko looked up from the batter he was mixing and nodded at an open door. There was a twisting staircase behind it, not a cupboard.

'Excellent.' Evrine walked in just in time to hear him. She found a stool and sat down as well. 'We can manage for the moment. We'll draw up a list of the things we need, and some letters of credit. You can take those back along the road with you, to give to merchants we know and trust.'

Toko paused in his stirring to drop dried apple into the bowl. 'Won't someone dispute your right to claim this place for your own?'

That was the thing about Toko, Lesh reflected. He didn't say much, but when he did, he could be as subtle as a smack in the mouth. To his relief, Evrine laughed.

'This is my great-grandfather's library. How else do you think I knew it was here to be found?' She waved that away. 'We won't have any problems.'

'Can I come back?' Lesh burst out. 'Can I bring your supplies? You'll still need someone to look after your mules and the horses.'

Toko looked at him, open-mouthed. 'Don't you want to go home? What do I tell Mam and Da?'

'I'll come home with you, of course I will, but – ' Lesh struggled to find the right words. 'But not to stay. Not now I've seen – everything we've seen. Now I know there's so much more to be seen.'

'You'll always be welcome here,' Sayesta glanced at Toko. 'Both of you, for however long you like.'

'Absolutely,' Evrine agreed. 'Now, how soon will those griddle cakes be ready?'

'Any moment.' Toko went over to the fireplace and carefully greased the hot iron with a scrap of lard on the point of his knife.

'Let's heat some water for tea.' Evrine stood up.

Sayesta rose to her feet as well. Lesh wasn't sure exactly what happened, but somehow between them, they jarred the table. Toko had left the bowl of batter too close to the edge. It teetered and fell to smash on the flagstones. At least, it would have smashed, only Sayesta flicked her hand. The bowl righted itself and sprang up to sit safely in the middle of the table.

Lesh stared, gaping. Then he closed his mouth and squared his shoulders. Now he knew he had made the right decision. The only question could be how many more wonders he might see. They might have reached the end of this road. This might be where Evrine and Sayesta chose to end their tale. Lesh knew beyond all doubt that his story was just beginning.

Juliet E. McKenna is Albedo One's preeminent book reviewer

The Vanishing Act

John Kenny

The child's head whips back, blond hair flying. Arms, small and skinny, pinwheel in the air, trying to grip at nothing. He falls to the floor of the sitting-room, his friends parting around him in order not to hinder his progress. The birthday party grinds to a halt and a prolonged silence of disbelief stifles the air.

I stand towering over the boys in top hat and tails, wand pointing to nowhere in one hand, a hot stinging pulse warming the other. My two cases of magic tricks stand open on fold out picnic chairs behind me. There is time to relive the preceding half hour, time to pick at it as the moment stretches.

The trudge up the gravel driveway from my beaten thirty-year-old Cortina hauling the heavy cases, the big house, the cars parked out front, the sound of screeching kids laughing and shouting piercing the red brick walls. The birthday boy's mother, I presume, answering the door, tall, sleek, maxi dress hinting at the pleasures to be had underneath, make-up perfect, blonde hair tied loosely back, half full glass of wine in one hand. The barest vestige of a smile cracking the corners of her mouth as she points me towards a room beside the main arena of festivities.

The clown has finished; they're having pizza now. She glides off into a large bright modern kitchen with a half dozen or so parents standing around a marble-topped island sipping vino and exchanging pleasantries.

I enter the room to get ready, a utility room, with washing machine, dryer, airing cupboards, wash baskets piled with clothes. Slumped in one corner is the clown, a bloom of orange curls crowning his head, Day-Glo paint plastering his face, stripy T-shirt and hoop-waisted ballooning trousers, flipper-like red shoes at a ninety degree angle to each other.

I register the naggin of whisky gripped in one hand, a cigarette in the other. The man is a wreck, the accoutrements of his trade strewn on the floor.

He straightens, no doubt aware of my distaste even through the fog of alcohol. He mumbles an excuse, and jerks the naggin in my direction, perhaps in the hope of enlisting me as a co-conspirator. I hesitate. Temptation flashes through me, the prospect of the neat golden liquid burning a track down my gullet and setting up a warm glow in my stomach quickening my blood. But an equally powerful surge of nausea dizzies me at the idea of associating with this riff raff.

Of course it's the drink that has brought me to this day. It's not fair, not remotely fair that the Magic Circle has seen fit to discharge me from its membership, casting me from the shelter of its respectability, its mutual admiration, and sense of honour.

'You'll need it with them shower of little bastards in there,' the clown urges. 'Fuck-you big house, how are ya. The state of the cars out there, too. Beemers, Jags, SUVs for the yummy mummys. I ask ya, what the fuck do they need four-wheel drives for in anyways? To get to the gym? I had to get the fuckin' bus here.'

He waves the bottle at me again. 'Go on.' I take it, wipe its lip, and down a swift swig of the amber liquid. The clown takes the bottle, caps it, and puffing on his cigarette, he scoops his stuff from the floor and jams it into a large canvas bag.

The noise level goes up a notch next door. The pizzas have been demolished; entertainment is demanded.

The clown wishes me luck as he flip flops from the room, canvas bag over his shoulder, a deep phlegmy cough his parting gesture.

Standing at the door, I steel myself, and open it on a scene of chaos. Kids screech at my arrival, rubbing against my nerve ends like a cheese grater. But there is no sense of anticipation in their cries, just an anarchic mayhem. Several boys seem unable to stop running about the room, colliding with chairs and the table, on which rests the half-eaten remains of their food. Popcorn and crisps lie scattered across the carpet, mashed in by eager feet. *7-Up* and *Coke* form pools on the plastic tablecloth. Balloons and streamers have been pulled from the walls.

I unfold the picnic chairs and open the cases, boys crashing into me and my paraphernalia as I try to set up my first trick. The birthday boy runs around me, chased by three other boys, all immune to dizziness.

I shout to be heard over the din. The birthday boy pauses to size me up. I can see a malicious glint in his eye, see that this is going to be little more than an endurance test.

The first trick, stuffing a handkerchief into my balled fist, then extracting it to reveal an endless line of handkerchiefs knotted together.

'Boring,' shouts the birthday boy, and everyone laughs.

I set up tubular containers to perform the disappearing bottle trick and the birthday boy knocks them over, revealing the inner workings of the vanishing act. 'Ha!' he pronounces, 'that's how it's done.'

I move on to the next trick. He says it's stupid. 'Any moron could do that.' The boy's friends get jittery again, the sugar from their fizzy drinks kicking in. They jump up and down, pull at each other, shove to the ground, and throw arm-deadening punches.

I shouldn't be here. I am, first and foremost, a prestidigitator, studied in the fine art of illusion and once respected by my peers, now reduced to the circumstances of a mere magician, purveyor of cheap tricks, with little or no finesse, to snotty little brats.

The birthday boy runs behind me and starts yanking at the tails of my coat. This sets the boys off. I swat him away and he trips over one of the cases, spilling everything on the floor.

The party turns into a smash and grab as boys loot my magic box of tricks and tear about the room waving the various colourful plastic knick-knacks. All authority is gone, if it ever existed, and I hare around after the boys, trying to regain my property.

A little of my hastily eaten lunch, half digested, pushes up from my stomach and I swallow it again, my mouth and throat stinging from its acidic taste. I think of Helen telling me this is the end. To get out. And Sophie a witness to it, a witness to the failure that is her father. The bed-

The clown wishes me luck as he flip flops from the room, canvas bag over his shoulder, a deep phlegmy cough his parting gesture.

sit, at fifty years of age. Christ; the little gas hob, the tiny wardrobe, the single creaky bed, the other tenants, all at college, in their early twenties, with lives of promise ahead of them.

The birthday boy sets up a call for ice cream. Most of the boys stop dashing around and join in the chant. I return to my spot and throw what I've managed to reclaim into the righted case. Perhaps a card trick.

As I turn to address the audience, to restore order and resume my act, the birthday boy takes a run at me, head down, straight at my stomach. He stops short, but I stumble back in panic, fall over the second case of tricks, chair, case and magical objects flying every which way.

I lie there in a daze, the noise of the kids receding as I bury myself in the past. Despised Helen, Helen the cause of it all, turning Sophie against me, the drink, the warming drink, the cold, lonely nights, the lack of respect, the shame. It all washes through me like a dose of *Andrews Liver Salts*.

I disentangle myself from the detritus and attempt to stand. A pain lances through my stomach, the warm whisky boiling about, seeking escape. I hold the boy by the shoulders in front of me, the room beginning to swirl before me, little black floaters dancing across my vision.

The birthday boy standing before me, who will coast through life, part of a network of the privileged, expensive grinds to help him pass muster in school, pushed through college, handed a top job in Daddy's firm, the fine looking girlfriend, the apartment paid for, the car covered by company expenses. The birthday boy standing before me with victory in his eyes.

The intake of breath for his last insult before ice cream, my hand reaching back, not a part of me, swinging about, connecting with his face. The child's head whips back, blond hair flying, the arms pin-wheeling the air as he falls to the floor.

The stunned silence, for a heartbeat blessed, before the terrible consequences rush in. The resumption of chaos, the shouts, the screams, the mother standing before me, face creased in anger, the father shouting, pulling me from the room. The Guards arriving, being eased, none too gently, into the back of the patrol car, pulling away from the big house and flashy cars, the group of distressed parents gathered on the gravel driveway disappearing from view as we reach the main road.

And in the silence of the patrol car as we speed towards the nearest Garda station, I gaze out the window in a dream of resignation, past pain and bitterness, and notice, sitting at a bus stop coming up, the clown, still in full regalia. The clown looks up and right at me, and as we pass him, that look betrays no recognition, not the slightest hint of understanding or brotherhood. It is blank. Inscrutable.

John Kenny is a founding editor of Albedo One.

www.albedo1.com

Colophon

Published by **Albedo One Productions** and copyright © 2023. Copyright reverts to contributors on publication.

Submissions
We are no longer looking for submissions.

Subscriptions
We request subscribers with issues promised after issue 50 who would like a refund to contact us at bobn91454@hotmail.com with their details.

Back Issues
Write us at 8 Bachelor's Walk, Dublin 1, Ireland, or much more conveniently at bobn91454@hotmail.com to let us know which issues you're looking for.

Editorial Team
Managing Editor: Robert Neilson
Associate Editors: Dev Agarwal and Sharon Kae Reamer
Contributing Editors: George Anderson, Jacqui Adams, Jon Del Arroz, Penelope Gollop, Wayne J. Harris, Terry Jackman, Roderick MacDonald, Juliet E. McKenna, John Moran, Christopher Morris and Konstantine Paradias.
Consulting Editors: John Kenny, David Murphy and Roelof Goudriaan.
Cover Art: Robert Neilson and AI-AI
Spot Art: Roelof Goudriaan, using Dream AI with sampled public domain artworks.

Editorial Address
Albedo One, 8 Bachelor's Walk, Dublin 1, Ireland. bobn91454@hotmail.com.

(left column: two rejected cover drafts)
ISBN 9798862025880

Printed in Poland
by Amazon Fulfillment
Poland Sp. z o.o., Wrocław